The
CLASSIC CRIME
LIBRARY
#15

PASSPORT TO PERIL

LAWRENCE BLOCK

writing as Anne Campbell Clark

The Classic Crime Library

*Available in paperback from Hard Case Crime

Chapter 1

Ellen Cameron sat uncomfortably upon a plastic-covered stool at the steel-and-Formica counter of one of the Forte's restaurants on the northeast side of Piccadilly Circus. She stirred a spoonful of sugar into her tea and set the spoon in the saucer beside the cup. She searched her purse for cigarettes, frowning when she found that there was only one left in the pack that she had opened that morning. She never smoked that heavily—it was bad for her voice. And at this rate the single carton of American cigarettes she had brought along would not last her even two weeks. She poked the cigarette back into the pack and returned the pack to the purse, sipped at her tea, drummed her fingers nervously upon the countertop, then gave up and dug out the cigarette once more and lit it.

She was a slender girl, medium-tall, her oval face framed with shoulder-length black hair. Her large eyes were a surprising blue. A few years ago at college a boy had told her that she should have posed for Modigliani. "But I wasn't even born then," she told him.

"Like Miniver Cheevy," he had said, "born too late."

Perhaps, she thought now, he had been right. Perhaps she had been improperly planted in time; perhaps she would better have belonged in a slower, more leisurely world. She looked around the restaurant, wincing at the brightness of it, the glare of the overhead light fixtures, the harshness of all the gleaming stainless steel, the impersonal efficiency of the waitresses, all of whom looked quite alike. She had grown accustomed to this sort of atmosphere in New York but found it quite unbearable in London. It clashed with her original image of the city, like Mod clothes and eye shadow on one's grandmother.

She sipped at her tea and put out her cigarette in a round glass ashtray. The same boy who had likened her to Miniver Cheevy had some weeks later been on the verge of proposing marriage; with just the slightest encouragement he would have. And she had been very careful not to offer any such encouragement.

Brian Ellery. What had happened to him since college? She knew bits and pieces of the answer, the sort of empty facts that appear in alumni bulletins. He had married, of course; when a young man makes up his mind to marry, the actual selection of a particular girl is secondary. He had decided to marry, and he had virtually decided to marry Ellen Cameron, and before very long he had instead married someone else. He and his wife had a child, perhaps two, and he was working for a large firm in Cleveland and living in some suburb. She did not remember precisely what he did, something to do with transportation rates or such. It had not sounded especially interesting.

> *I never shall marry*
> *I'll be no man's wife*
> *I'm bound to stay single*
> *All the days of my life*

The old Irish ballad ran through her mind, and she smiled at it. She did not sing it often any more (*Make of that*, she thought, *what you will!*) but had included it on the first of her two albums for Folklore Records. *I never shall marry . . .*

It was ridiculous, she thought, for her to act as though that dismal dirge was her unofficial theme song. She was only twenty-four and hardly an irredeemable old maid. America might be overflowing with featherheaded women who were wives at seventeen and grandmothers at thirty-five, but that hardly meant that she was over the hill. She had never honestly regretted not having married Brian Ellery. Though an interesting boy, he had seemed predestined to grow into a dull man, and he would have irresistibly transformed her into a dull woman. She could not be sorry for having given him up. Only at moments like this, when she felt unusually alone and oppressively wrapped up in herself, did her mind begin to concern itself with What Might Have Been.

She put out her cigarette. As his wife, she thought, she would have found herself seeking out premature middle age in some drab suburb. Her guitar would have gathered dust in the attic, her singing voice would have atrophied and—to bend melodrama into farce—her name would have been absurdly changed to Ellen Ellery.

She left a shilling and three pence on the counter and moved from the glare of the restaurant to the glare of Piccadilly. It was her last night in London. In the morning she would fly to Dublin. Now, though it was near midnight, she did not much want to return to her hotel. She ached to go somewhere, to do something exciting. She had expected far more from London than the city had given her, and now, with her stay almost over, she felt that she was being cheated.

The play she had seen that evening might have been partly responsible for her mood. It was very crisp and dry and brittle, a humorless comedy of adultery and incest and sexual inversion that had drawn inexplicable peals of laughter from the people around Ellen. She had not laughed once and had come very close to leaving after the second act. It was not that it had shocked her or that she was the sort of theatergoer who prefers the facile ebullience of a musical comedy to the drama of a more demanding play. But the barrenness of *Drums for Portia* had echoed the vacant quality of the week she had spent in London, and the final effect was desperately depressing.

She started toward a queue of taxis. She found the huge black British cabs charming, just as she had found the tour of the Tower of London a moving encounter with the presence of History, just as she also found enchantment in quiet walks through the still streets of Bloomsbury around her hotel. There was nothing really *wrong* with the city, she told herself. The failure was probably her own; she was not fitting into things, not responding to stimuli that should have been more genuinely stimulating than they were. She was in the city but not of it, and thus she was being bored and repelled by the very aspects of London that might otherwise have fascinated her.

She turned away from the cabs, changing her mind suddenly. It was, after all, her last night in London. There seemed to be nowhere for her to go, no one she might visit, no nightclub she could attend unescorted; but at the same time there was no need for her to rush back to Crichton Hall in a taxi. It was a fine September night, the air just a shade on the cool side, the sky quite clear, the stars bright in a moonless sky. She decided to walk back to the hotel. Her map was in her other purse, but she didn't expect to get lost and could always take a taxi later on if her feet tired. At least she was on the right side of Piccadilly and wouldn't have to fight her way through the traffic.

She walked along Shaftesbury Avenue for several blocks, then turned left on Frith Street and found herself moving through the narrow streets of Soho. She had been in the section several times by day, but this was her first experience of it at night. It was different now. In daylight, it had appeared as it had been described to her, an English equivalent of Greenwich Village, with its book shops and Italian restaurants and quaint pubs. Now it revealed a sordid quality that had not been evident in the brighter light of day. Girls and more girls, their faces cluttered with makeup, their opulent bodies stuffed into overtight clothing, lounged purposefully in doorways or called seductively from their windows to passing males. Ferret-faced little men sought out obvious tourists, caught at their arms, whispered furtively into their ears. Helmeted bobbies walked the dark streets in pairs, moving as if aware of an oppressive atmosphere of incipient violence. Doorways held little thumbtacked notices on three-by-five index cards.

FRENCH MODEL—MISS BIRCH
EXPERIENCED GOVERNESS
APT. 3-C. FRENCH LESSONS, INQUIRE WITHIN.

She quickened her pace, kept her eyes fixed straight ahead, tried not to notice the endless supply of girls who displayed themselves in what struck her as a cynical caricature of femininity. She had the feeling that someone was following her, that she had been mistaken for one of these flashy denizens of Soho. At least she had left her white purse at home in New York. That was one of the badges of these girls, she had read. A large white purse and a belted trench coat. Though none of these girls seemed to be outfitted in that fashion. Perhaps the book she had read was out of date. Perhaps styles changed, even in that profession.

It was absurd, but she couldn't shake off the feeling that she was being followed. Involuntarily she found herself stopping, darting glances over her shoulder. Was it her imagination, or did a male face seem to shrink back from her gaze, melting away from her eyes into the shadows and doorways?

Of course it was her imagination. She was turning into a typical old maid; she would get to her room at Crichton Hall and look under the bed for burglars. Why would anyone follow her through Soho? There were certainly enough other women available for anyone so inclined.

> *I never shall marry*
> *I'll be no man's wife*

She stopped to get a cigarette, then remembered that she had finished the pack at Forte's. She resumed walking, still unable to shake the feeling that there was someone behind her. At Soho Square, she found herself carefully skirting the little park as if it were Central Park in New York, unsafe for walking after dark. It was absurd, and she recognized the absurdity of it, but she could not seem to help herself.

She rounded the tiny park, walked to New Oxford Street, and turned east again. Her feet were beginning to hurt. It seemed as though she had spent all her time in London walking from one place to another, walking through the British Museum and the Tower and Westminster Abbey, walking to the theater, walking endlessly. She turned to look for a cab, and again she had the feeling that someone had been following her, that a man or two men had melted into the shadows as she turned.

There were no cabs in sight. It was only a few more blocks, she told herself, just a little further to the small bed-and-breakfast house on Bedford Place off Russell Square. Her feet could certainly hold out. And she knew that she was using her tired feet as an excuse for her mind, that it was the unholy feeling of being pursued that made her anxious to take a cab. She did not intend to let herself behave like an idiot. She would walk home, it was a beautiful night, there was no one behind her . . .

There was someone behind her.

She was just two blocks from her hotel, two blocks and a few odd houses, when she knew that her feeling was more than a feeling, that there actually was someone behind her. She heard footsteps, neatly fitted to her own but still discernible. She quickened her pace, and the footsteps to her rear speeded up in response. She turned her head, looked across the street, and saw that there was a man in the shadows on the other side of the street as well, walking at the same speed, walking behind her.

Before, she had been anxious. Now she was terrified. Fear

leaped up within her, a physical presence, cold, brittle, pressing painfully within her chest and pushing at the base of her throat. She couldn't seem to catch her breath. Her hands hardened into small fists, and their palms went moist with the cool, stale sweat of terror. She wanted to run, but that would only make them run after her, and she knew they could catch her. She walked faster, looking involuntarily over her shoulder, and again saw the man across the street. This time he saw that she saw him.

He stepped out from the curb into the street. For the shadow of a second she caught a glimpse of him in the half light of a streetlamp, a very tall knife-thin man, his nose long and prominent, his shoulders hunched forward in an attitude of pursuit.

Now she started to run, turning from the men behind her, feet working furiously on the pavement. She was almost at the corner when she stumbled and fell. She threw her hands out to break the fall, and her purse dropped to the ground. She grabbed it up, regained her feet, darted across the street, started to fall again, caught her balance, began to run once more—and then they had her.

Two of them, there were two of them, and they both reached her at once. A hand touched her shoulder and chilled her to the bone. She froze, and the hand spun her around, and she opened her mouth to scream—and why hadn't she screamed at the start, why, why?—but no sound came from her lips, nothing at all. The tall man was holding her, and the shorter man, the one she had not seen before, was reaching out to her. Fingers dug cruelly into her shoulder. Her mouth opened again, and this time she would have screamed, but a hand was clapped over her mouth and no sound could get past it.

Hands tore her purse from her grasp. Other hands pressed at the back of her neck, a firm, insistent pressure. Her legs were suddenly boneless, limp. She gasped for breath. Her eyes slid shut, and her brain burned bloody red. The red went to gray, the gray to black.

Hands released her, and she fell slowly, slowly, to the pavement.

Chapter 2

"Easy, now. Don't be trying to get up too quickly, Miss. Take nice deep breaths, they'll clear your head. Fainted, did you?"

She opened her eyes and looked up into the kindly florid face of a middle-aged woman with bright red hair and small bright eyes. "Two men," she said. "They were following me, and" —she touched the back of her neck experimentally, her fingers finding only the slightest trace of soreness— "and one of them tried to choke me. I thought I was going to be killed."

"And in this neighborhood! I don't know what the city's coming to. Got a mugger's hold on you, did he? And I'd guess you had a purse and that it's gone now."

She got to her knees, then rose to her feet. She looked around for her purse, then remembered the hands that had eased it from her grasp. "A small black evening bag," she said. "It doesn't seem to be here."

"No, and small chance you'll see it again. You're from America? We have a few of your programs on the telly, you know. Suppose you're used to this sort of thing. My flat's just next door, I was just out to take the midnight air. Are you up to walking a bit? Come in with me, you'll feel fitter after a cup of tea."

"Oh, I'm all right . . ."

"Come in and sit for a bit," the woman said. "You don't

want to be alone now. There's shock that sets in after any-thing of the sort, even just a bit of purse snatchery, and you wouldn't want to be by yourself. Are you staying nearby?"

"Just two blocks from here. Crichton Hall."

"I know the hotel. It's cozy there, isn't it? But sit with me for ten minutes, and then you'll feel more up to going home to bed."

Ellen considered. She did need company, and the woman was pleasant, someone to talk to. She nodded gratefully, and the red-haired woman led her into the house next door and up a flight of stairs to her flat. "I really can't stay long," Ellen said. "I have to get up early in the morning to catch a plane."

"Where are you going?"

"Dublin."

"Oh, I've never been, but from what I've heard you'll like it there. Will you be spending much time in Ireland?"

"Almost two weeks." The woman brought the tea, and Ellen added milk and sugar to hers. "About what happened," she said. "Do you suppose I ought to call the police?"

"Well, you're supposed to report it. Did you lose much money?"

"Hardly anything. My traveler's checks are in my other purse, and most of my cash. Oh, my passport! No, that's all in my other purse. I was a little anxious about that, I remember, because they tell you to carry it with you wherever you go, but I didn't bother changing it from one purse to the other. I suppose it's lucky I didn't."

"You'd be up against it otherwise, losing your passport. They'd never let you on the plane tomorrow."

"Then it was lucky. No, I only had about ten pounds with me, less the theater ticket and what I spent for dinner. Maybe seven pounds. I don't suppose there's any chance I'll get it back."

The woman shook her head. "Not unless a bobby caught them right in the act, and of course they didn't. If it's only the seven pounds and nothing else is involved, I wouldn't ring up the police if I were you. More trouble than it's worth, really. They won't catch the rogues, and they'll only ask you dozens of questions and make you look at photographs. I know a woman friend of mine had a burglar into her rooms, took a coat and some jewelry, and of course she had to report it for the insurance. Said it was barely worth it, though she did collect from the insurance company. But all the questions they asked, and you do want to get your sleep and be on your plane in the morning. Poor child, what a way to spend your last night in London! What will you think of our city?"

When Ellen finished her tea, she said that she really ought to be going back to her hotel, and the woman insisted on walking with her. "I'm sure I'll be all right," she said, but the woman said that she wanted a bit of fresh air anyway and that Ellen no doubt had her nerves on edge and shouldn't be walking in the dark by herself. They walked the two blocks together, and Ellen let herself in with her key and went up to her room.

She was tired but knew she would be unable to fall asleep right away. She opened a fresh pack of American cigarettes, lit one, drew deeply on it, and set it down in a small triangular ashtray that carried an advertisement for Guinness Stout. She got her suitcase from the closet, propped it open on the bed, and began packing. All the guide books had emphasized the advisability of traveling light, and she had taken their advice, taking a bare minimum of clothes and fitting everything into a single suitcase. Even so she had had to pay extra charges on the airplane for her guitar and her tape recorder.

Her packing completed, she sat down in the Victorian armchair and went through her purse. What a stroke of luck it had been, taking the smaller bag to the theater and neglecting to transfer the passport and health certificate and traveler's checks! She still had everything she needed, including her ticket to Dublin and her other tickets, one from Shannon to Berlin and another from Berlin back to New York.

Guiltily, she lit a second cigarette from the butt of the first and sat back, smoking nervously. It was only natural, she thought; she was still shaky from the purse snatching—and at the time it had seemed that they might be after far more than her near-empty purse. She blew out a cloud of smoke, and her eyes followed it on its way to the ceiling. When she finished the cigarette she sat back in the chair and closed her eyes and thought about the odd combination of events that had brought her to London . . .

It had begun with a fearfully official envelope with DEPARTMENT OF STATE in its upper left-hand corner. The letter inside explained that she had been selected to represent the United States at the Third International Festival of Folk Music and Dancing, to be held in West Berlin during the second week of October. While she would receive no fee for her performance, the United States Government would be pleased to reimburse her for first-class air passage to and from Berlin, and the West German Government would provide her with food and lodging during the week of the festival. She would be required to accept or reject the invitation within ten days and to submit to the State Department, in triplicate, a tentative program of ten songs that she would be prepared to perform during the festival competition.

The invitation had thrilled her. While other events were considerably more important in the world of folk music, the Berlin festival was internationally recognized and carried a certain amount of prestige. And she would be going to it as one of the American representatives. The honor of having been selected would benefit her professionally, and the chance to travel was even more exciting. She wrote back at once, submitting a detailed program of the songs she would sing and expressing her delight at having been chosen.

Her agent was as happy as she was. "This is a big break for you, Ellen," he told her. "You've been getting nothing but small stuff, the minor folk-music clubs in the Village, a couple of concerts, college campus dates. Your albums are good, and Folklore is happy with them, but it's no secret that they're setting no sales records. This'll give us a good publicity hook. Don't kid yourself—all it amounts to is that you got on a list that the cultural exchange people in Washington are using. But I ought to be able to get you some good bookings on the strength of it." He pursed his lips, regarding her thoughtfully. "Do you just want to hop to Berlin and back? Or would you like to make a trip out of it?"

"What do you mean?"

"You'll see," he said.

And he showed her what he meant. With nothing more than the State Department invitation to back him up, he had gone to Folklore Records and persuaded them to pick up the tab for a few weeks in England and Ireland. "They've done very well with Irish ballads lately," he told her. "They'll pay your expenses to travel through Ireland gathering material. Go right through the country, stop in the small towns, take your tape recorder, and get yourself some fresh material. When you come back you'll have enough for an album, and they'll go for the album. Maybe even two albums..."

"And I could record some material by native singers," she suggested. "They might want that for their Ethnic series. Ballads in Gaelic. I could..."

He smiled. "You're getting the idea now. That's not all. You'll go to London first. I'm pretty sure I can book you into a pair of concerts there. The pay won't be the best in the world, but it should more than cover your expenses. And then when you come back we'll have a lot of selling points to back you up with. 'Ellen Cameron, recently returned from a tour of Western Europe with triumphal appearances in London and Berlin, performing her repertoire of folk ballads unearthed in the hamlets of Western Ireland.' You'll get a Town Hall booking out of that one, and possibly even Carnegie, though I wouldn't guarantee it."

"It sounds fantastic."

He grinned. "You see what it is, Ellen? It isn't enough to be good. You're a good singer, your voice is smooth and strong and you handle it well, and it's a fact that your guitar playing is a good two hundred percent better than it was two years ago. But that's not enough. They have to know you, they have to know your name and your face and what you've done and who you are. Once you start to establish yourself, everything you do helps everything else. Your albums bring people to the concerts, and your concerts help sell record albums, and suddenly you begin to make it. It doesn't happen overnight. It takes time, but time is something you have plenty of, a young kid like you, and this trip could be a big help to you."

"I can hardly wait. How long would I be gone altogether?"

"Say a week in London and two or three weeks in Ireland. Then a week in Berlin and then home. So figure a month altogether."

"It sounds heavenly."

"Don't expect luxury, unless you've got money of your own stashed away. Do you?"

She thought of the years since college, the years of working at odd jobs, picking up a little money at concerts, occasional payments for recording sessions. It was remarkable that she had managed to stay out of debt. She had never been able to set any money aside.

"No," she said.

"Then you won't be living high. You wouldn't want to anyway, not if you want to go among the people and collect new songs. You'll stay in inexpensive hotels and eat at cheap restaurants. But it should be fun for you. You've never been out of the country before?"

"Never."

"I think you'll enjoy it."

"I know I will."

And she would, she thought fiercely. True, London had been a disappointment, but London was only a small portion of the trip. She had had two bookings in London, and they had not added up to what she had hoped for. The first concert turned out to be more rock 'n' roll than true folk music, and they had let her sing only three songs, toward the end of the show. The audience, while polite, was generally unresponsive.

The second concert, because of some fluke, had been

canceled entirely. The folk singers she had hoped to see in London—a trio she had met in New York and the only persons in England she knew well enough to speak with—had picked that particular week to fly to New York. So she'd been stranded, friendless and alone, in a city that had been less than kind to her. The sightseeing and the theater had not made up for all of this. Now the purse snatching was the crowning blow, the finishing touch.

No matter, she told herself. London, after all, was the least important part of her trip. Tomorrow she would be off for Dublin, and then she would have days on end to spend touring Ireland with tape recorder and guitar. With any luck at all she would return with enough material on tape for half a dozen albums. True folk songs, sprung from the hearts of the Irish people and passed on from generation to generation as part of a vibrant oral tradition and heritage.

She got undressed, laid out clothes for the morning, and got into bed. She pulled the covers over her and settled her head on the soft feather pillow.

For a moment the memory of pursuit in the dark London streets came back to her in a flash. The man, moving into the glow of the streetlamp, his features sharp and terrifying. Running, and slipping, and being caught. The firm grip on the back of her neck, the dull pain, slipping, falling, the world turning black . . .

But it was over now. She took a deep breath and closed her eyes, certain that it would be hours before she could sleep; and then, surprisingly, sleep came in a rush.

*   *   *

Her travel alarm woke her at eight. It rang so softly that she almost slept through it, but she awoke in time, rubbed the sleep from her eyes, slipped into her trench coat ("Use your raincoat in place of a bathrobe," the guide books had suggested, "and save room in your suitcase."), and walked down the hall to the communal bathroom. She bathed quickly, thinking again how odd it was to be charged for every bath you took. The price was just a shilling, only fourteen cents, but it did seem odd to pay extra to be clean.

In her room, she dressed quickly and went down the stairs for breakfast. Crichton Hall served an excellent breakfast, three eggs and sausages and juice and cereal and toast and a pot of tea. She shared a table with two spinster ladies from France who spoke French to one another and ignored Ellen entirely. When she finished breakfast she asked the landlady to prepare her bill and call a taxi.

She paid her bill, got her suitcases from her room, and took the taxi to the airport bus terminal. The cab driver offered to take her straight to the airport, but she was afraid the ride would cost too much. She rode to the bus terminal instead and took the bus to the airport. She checked her suitcase and guitar and decided to carry her tape recorder onto the plane with her. It was a small model, fully transistorized and not too heavy but good enough to record music faithfully.

Sitting on a bench in the airport, the tape recorder on her knees, she wondered if that might be one of the reasons she had felt ill at ease in London. Here she was, with her tape recorder and her guitar, and she hadn't been putting either of them to good use yet. In Ireland things would be different. She could picture herself in the singing pubs in Dublin or in the counties in the south and west, Tipperary and Cork and

Kerry, seeking out the native singers and learning new songs and getting exciting new material on tape. She was anxious to get to work, anxious to be doing what she had come across the ocean to do.

Soon, she thought. *Soon.*

She went through exit customs, had her passport stamped, and moved into another room to wait for her Aer Lingus flight to be called. everyone was very polite. The young man who stamped her exit visa on her passport gave her a big smile. "Off to Ireland, are you?"

"Yes," she said.

"Well, you'll like it there. Come back and visit us again, will you?"

"Oh, I will," she said. And she knew that she would. Her disappointment with London, she decided, had been a very personal thing, an unfair judgment of a great and grand city. The coldness and impersonality of it could be balanced off by some very fine things, she knew. The sweet red-haired woman who had helped her last night, the gentle civility of the passport clerk, the efficient politeness that had greeted her everywhere she had gone. And the fine breakfasts at Crichton Hall, and the sense of History echoing in ancient streets. Yes, she thought, she would be back.

Her flight was called. She got to her feet, followed a herd of passengers through a flight gate and out toward a sleek green-trimmed jet. A stewardess, looking trim and pretty in the Kelly-green uniform of the Irish international airline, welcomed her and the rest of the passengers aboard in English just faintly touched with a melodious Irish brogue. Then she repeated the welcome in Gaelic.

Ellen drank in the words, savoring the texture of the

Gaelic tongue. She had heard the old Irish language sung—indeed, she could sing two or three songs in Irish—but she had never heard the language spoken before. She would have to hear a great deal of it, she decided. She couldn't hope to learn it, but if she let her ear grow accustomed to the sound of the language it would be much easier for her to render Irish songs effectively.

She sat by the window. The plane was still filling with passengers for the nonstop flight to the Irish capital. She looked out the window at the crowds of people boarding and leaving other planes. It was a busy airport, even busier than Kennedy.

"I beg your pardon, Miss. Is this seat taken?"

She turned at the voice. A tall man was bending over her. His hair was dark, and he wore the turned collar and black robes of a Catholic priest. He was in his late thirties, she guessed, though she had always found it hard to tell the ages of clergymen. There was something ageless about them, some quality that set them apart.

"No, it's not taken," she said. "Please sit down."

He sat beside her, buckled his seatbelt, and sighed. "Ah, it's a beautiful day for flying," he said. "And are you going home to Dublin this morning?"

"I'm going to Dublin, but it's not my home. I'm an American."

"I've never been to America, but it's a second home to many an Irishman. I've relatives in Boston and Philadelphia, and family on my mother's side in Chicago, as well. What part of America are you from?"

"New York."

"And might I ask if you're of Irish descent?"

She smiled. "Partly, I think. My name is Cameron and my

mother's maiden name was Paisley. Cameron is Scottish, of course, but I think the first Paisleys came from Northern Ireland. Though our family has been in America for so long that that's all we are now, really. American."

"It must be a grand country."

"It is." She hesitated. "Though I've never been anywhere else, until this trip. I've had a wonderful time in London" —it was a small enough lie— "and I'm very anxious to see Ireland."

"Ah, no more so than I myself." He shook his head sadly. "I've been three years in Africa, and you can't know how glad I'll be to get back to my own land. Not that I'm not glad for the opportunity to do the Lord's work, but I'd be just as happy if the Lord could find some work for me to do in County Clare." His eyes twinkled. "And I hope you'll forgive me that little touch of blasphemy. But three years in Tanzania leaves a man lonesome for his own native soil."

"What did you do there, exactly?"

"We had a small mission in a town not far from Dar es Salaam. That's the capital of the country, you know. There were two countries at first, Tanganyika and Zanzibar, but the two merged. Both were British colonies originally and it's not very hard for an Irishman to sympathize with other peoples who have spent some time beneath the British flag. We ran a small Jesuit mission in the town and brought the faith to those of the natives who were anxious to receive it. And brought medicines and a bit of education to the others. Oh, it was an exciting experience, to be sure."

The engines warmed up, and the plane taxied down a long runway, then took off into the wind. She sat in her seat and listened intently as the soft-spoken priest told of his experiences in the small African village. She hadn't realized until then how starved she was for conversation. It was a delight to listen to his gentle Irish speech, and she found herself hanging on every word.

He told her of the primitive superstitions of the natives and of the crude and often squalid lives they led. He talked of assisting a woman in childbirth and the sense of pride he had felt later on officiating at the infant's christening. "It was a grand feeling," he said, "for the Reverend Michael Farrell, S.J."

"I can imagine it was."

"A moving experience." He smiled. "You're not a Catholic, are you, Ellen?"

"No, I'm not. How did you know?"

"You haven't called me *Father*. You may, you know, whether you're of the Catholic faith or not. It's what we're used to being called, you see. My villagers used to call me *Father Mike* almost religiously, and then they'd go to their tents and pray to their pagan gods quite as if I hadn't been there at all. But it's a pity you're not Catholic, because there's a Jesuit joke I'd very much like to try out on you, and lacking the background you might not be able to appreciate it."

"I'd be happy to hear it."

"Well, then, let me try. There were three good workers in the vineyard of the Lord, do you see, and one was a Dominican friar and another a Christian Brother and the third a Jesuit priest, and the three became caught up in a most unholy argument as to who was most important in the carrying out of the Lord's work. And each grew quite vehement over the whole affair, arguing that his particular order was highest in the Lord's eyes.

"Until suddenly, as the three stood arguing amongst themselves, the sky was split by a bolt of lightning and an earthshaking peal of thunder. And the three went all quiet, and a huge finger appeared and began writing upon the face of the sky. 'You must stop this foolish bickering,' the finger wrote. 'You are all equal in my sight. Whether Jesuits or Christian Brothers or Dominicans, you are all doing my work. Continue with the work of the Lord and cease wasting precious time in godless disputation.' And do you know how the holy message was signed?"

"How?"

"Why, it was signed, 'God, S.J.'"

She began to laugh, and Father Farrell smiled at her. "Now tell me," he said. "Is that joke funny to a non-Catholic? I know it's a story priests like to laugh at and that some Catholics would appreciate, but does it strike you funny?"

"Oh, yes," she assured him.

He told her another joke, this time in a richly comic Irish brogue, about an old woman smuggling whiskey home from a pilgrimage on the pretext that it was holy water. When the customs inspector tasted it and announced its actual character, the woman feigned astonishment.

"Saints be praised," came the punch line, "'tis a miracle!"

And, after she had relaxed in genuine laughter, he shook his head sadly and apologized for monopolizing the conversation. "Here I am talking away a mile a minute and not giving you a chance to say a word," he said. "When what I really ought to do is ask you where you'll be going in Ireland and what you plan to do here. Is it just a brief stop for you, or will you have time to see something of the country?"

"Oh, I'll be here for two or three weeks."

"Ah, how wonderful! Just in Dublin, or will you travel around?"

"I hope to travel a great deal."

He drew her out with more questions, and she found herself telling him everything about her trip, from the first letter from the State Department to the purse-snatching episode of the night before. He was an excellent listener, evidently genuinely interested in everything she had to say, and she discovered that she had missed the opportunity for real conversation. She told him that she planned to spend several days in Dublin and had made a reservation at a hotel in Amiens Street. After that, she planned to head south and west with no firm itinerary in mind. She wanted to make sure to get to the Festival of Kerry in Tralee and to move on to the tiny town of Dingle for the conclusion of the festival, but beyond that she had no hard-and-fast plans.

"I'll probably be traveling by bus," she said. "I'll just go from one town to the next and see what develops. What singers and songs I can unearth. I want to fill as many tapes as I possibly can."

"It's a fine country for it."

"So I understand."

"The ballad is a rich Irish tradition. To this day we have traveling balladeers, you know, men who go to the horse shows and the hurling matches and travel the whole course of the country making up songs about current events. They don't fulfill the function they once did, back in the days when ballads were the newspapers and radios of the common man, but they still exist."

"I know. And are there still Gypsies? I've read about them . . ."

"Gypsies? Oh, you mean the Irish Gypsies? The traveling people?"

"Yes."

"You still find them in the south and west, though not as many as there were in the past. They're not true Romany Gypsies, you know. They're Irish families who took to the roads when Cromwell's men evicted them from the land in the seventeenth century. You'll see them, with their pretty cylindrical wagons and their horses. Tinkers, we call them. Good at mending pots and pans, and good at emptying a jar of poteen. If you can meet them, you'll learn songs that have never found their way into songbooks."

"And do you think I could meet them?"

"It's a friendly country. You can meet anyone you've a mind to meet, Ellen."

They were still talking when the plane completed its passage over the Irish Sea and broke through the clouds for the descent to Dublin Airport. She looked out the window at the country spread out below and almost gasped at the vivid green of it. The ground was cut up by little fences into brilliant patches of green that were almost unreal in the intensity of their coloration.

"Now I understand," she said.

"What's that?"

"I knew it was green. I knew that was why they called it the Emerald Isle. All of that. But I never realized it looked like this."

He was craning his neck for a peek at his homeland. "Ireland," he said softly. "Isn't it beautiful?"

"Yes. Yes, it is."

The plane landed smoothly and taxied to a stop. The stewardess made another speech, this time welcoming them to Ireland, and repeated herself in Gaelic. Father Farrell helped

Ellen get her tape recorder from the overhead luggage rack, then followed her off the plane. The sun shone brightly from between the clouds overhead, and at the same time a gentle rain, scarcely more than a mist, was falling.

"Now I know that I'm home," he said. "It takes an Irish rain to make me certain of it. It always rains in Ireland, you know. Not even the sun can stop it. In Tanzania it was either hot and dry, or else the heavens opened up in a cloudburst. Here it always rains but never pours. You never drown and you're never dry."

In the airport, they queued up to wait for their luggage. Her suitcase turned up quickly, but when the last of the carts of luggage was brought in she still could not find her guitar.

"Oh, dear," she said. "I hope it wasn't left in London."

"I'm sure they'll find it."

"Oh, I suppose I could buy another if I have to, but I don't—oh, I hope . . ."

The priest laid a hand on her shoulder. "Now isn't this a fine way to welcome you to Ireland?" He took her arm. "Just let me make it a bit easier for you, my child. Let me have your passport and luggage checks, will you? And then you take yourself over to the counter there for a cup of hot tea, and by the time you've finished it I'll have your guitar for you. Just you relax and let me take care of everything for you."

She handed over her passport and luggage checks, then let him lead her to a lunch counter. She ordered two cups of tea, set one aside for Father Farrell, and added milk and sugar to her own. The tea was strong and rich, and she sat sipping it and wondering what could have happened to her guitar. What would she do if they couldn't find it? She had had the same guitar for almost four years, had paid almost a hundred dollars for it in a Third Avenue pawn shop, and had felt lucky to get it for that price. How could she replace it? And how could she possibly perform at Berlin with an inferior, unfamiliar instrument?

She had just about managed to get herself profoundly worked up over the matter, when the priest appeared, his own suitcase in one hand, her guitar in the other. She let out a great sigh of relief, then found herself laughing at her own discomfiture.

"You see?" he told her. "No problem at all. They were afraid it might be damaged in the regular luggage compartment, so they had it riding right up with us in the passenger area. It was probably no more than a few feet from us throughout the trip. Open the case, why don't you, and make sure that it's in good condition."

She unsnapped the case and took out the guitar. The fingers of her left hand automatically positioned themselves on the strings, and she strummed a few chords. "Out of tune," she said, "but that's nothing new. Close enough for folk music, anyway. That's a joke among folk singers."

"Not as private a joke as you might imagine. When the organ is a shade out of tune, we say it's close enough for the six o'clock mass."

"Really? I never heard that."

"And I never heard your version, but perhaps one private world is much like another. Here's your passport, you won't want to forget that. Oh, you ordered a cup of tea for me. That's kind of you. You can go straight through customs now, if you wish. Or if you care to wait, I'll make sure you get to your hotel."

"Oh, I'm sure I can get there without any trouble. I'll just take a taxi."

"Would you like me to come with you? If there's any trouble over your reservation, I might be able to help."

"I'm sure there won't be any trouble. And I wouldn't want to take you out of your way."

"I've plenty of time."

She got to her feet. "No, it's quite all right." She slung the guitar case over her shoulder, then picked up the tape recorder and the suitcase. "I do want to thank you," she said earnestly. "Not just for getting my guitar for me, but for being . . . oh, for being so very nice. I enjoyed our conversation very much."

"No more than I did, I assure you."

"Thank you. And I . . . I'm sure I'll love Ireland."

"I hope you do," he said. "Perhaps we'll see each other again. It's a small country, you know. A tiny little island. I'll be at home in County Clare, and I may get down to Kerry for a bit. I've friends and family there. We may encounter each other again before you leave."

"Oh, I hope so."

"And if not" —he smiled— "I do hope you enjoy your stay here. And I wish you all the luck in the world in Berlin."

Chapter 3

As she had expected, there was no trouble about her room. The woman at The White House, slender, with a heart-shaped face and a soft Dublin brogue, led her up a flight of stairs to a spacious room with a window facing out on Amiens Street. The price was a pound a day, with breakfast included. Ellen said that the room was fine and signed the guest register in the hall downstairs. She glanced over the other entries in the old ledger. Most of the guests were English, with a few Canadians and some Irish from cities like Cork and Galway. She was the first American to stay at The White House in almost three months.

She went to her room, unpacked, and took her guitar from its case. She struck a few chords, then went through the laborious process of tuning the instrument by ear. In the course of this her high E-string broke, and she had to replace it. Fortunately she had half a dozen spares for each of the six strings of the guitar. She had heard enough horror stories of performers stranded in out-of-the-way spots with a broken guitar string, and she was not likely to forget to carry a spare. A blues singer had told her of one such time, a nightclub date in East St. Louis. His G-string broke, and he replaced it, and the replacement snapped while he was tuning up. "And every store in town closed, and I didn't know another guitar player

within fifty miles." He had wound up playing the entire evening with five strings on the guitar.

"Ellen," he had told her, "I was about as good without
that G-string as a stripper would have been. Everybody in the
place got too drunk to know whether I was good or not, but
I was stone sober, and I heard everything I played, and you
better believe it was bad." So she had brought plenty of spares.
She might make her raincoat double in brass as a bathrobe,
and she might make do with only two purses and two dresses
and three skirt-and-sweater combinations, but her guitar was
going to stay in good shape.

She replaced the broken string, tuned it, kicked off her
shoes, sat on the very soft bed, and began to play. She closed
her eyes and let her fingers work on the strings without consciously selecting a tune. She had been playing the guitar for
almost ten years, and for almost half that time the instrument
had functioned as an extension of her own self. She had heard
all the jokes about folk musicians who took their instruments
to bed with them, about musicians who felt literally naked
when they left their guitars or banjos at home, and she knew
now that the jokes had a very real truth to them. She did feel
incomplete without the guitar. It was a part of her, one of her
private voices, and the thought of losing it at the airport, of
being forcibly parted from it, had held an almost surgical terror for her.

Her fingers picked out chords and melodies. She did not
select songs consciously but sat with her eyes closed and let
the guitar speak for her. She was in Dublin, and she thought
about the songs that had come out of Dublin, songs of the
Easter Rising of 1916, songs of an earlier rising in Dublin,

when a Dublin boy named Robert Emmet tried to start an insurrection in 1803, just five years after the glorious rebellion of '98. Spies and informers infiltrated his movement, and the British let it gather just enough momentum so that they could have an excuse to crush it once and for all, and hang Emmet in the bargain.

She remembered his speech from the dock. "I have but one request to ask at my departure from this world; it is the charity of silence. Let no man write my epitaph, for as no man who knows my motives dare now vindicate them, let not prejudice nor ignorance disperse them. Let them and me repose in obscurity and peace, and my tomb remain uninscribed, until other times and other men do justice to my character. When my country takes her place among the nations of the earth, then, and not until then, let my epitaph be written. I have done!"

And her fingers found the right notes, and she sang.

> *The battle is over, the boys are defeated*
> *Old Ireland's surrounded with sadness and gloom*
> *We were defeated and shamefully treated*
> *And I, Robert Emmet, awaiting my doom*
> *Hanged, drawn, and quartered, sure that was my*
>   *sentence*
> *But soon I will show them no coward am I*
> *My crime was the love of the land I was born in*
> *A hero I lived—and a hero I'll die . . .*

Later she changed her shoes and went downstairs for a walk and a bite of lunch. The woman with the heart-shaped face was dusting the tables in the parlor. "I heard you singing

'Robert Emmet,'" she said shyly. "I did not know that they knew our old songs in America."

"I know a few of them. I hope I didn't disturb you . . ."

"Surely you did not. And how would a song so sweetly sung disturb a person? He was a Dublin boy, Robert Emmet was. It was in Thomas Street that he rallied his men and in Thomas Street that they hanged him, and you could walk from here to there in half an hour. My father used to sing that very song, him and my uncles. And 'Kevin Barry,' but of course you know that one, don't you?"

"Yes."

"And doesn't everyone know 'Kevin Barry'? There was a time you couldn't turn on the radio without hearing it, unless it was the BBC you were listening to. Not likely you'd hear it there!" She laughed. "And the song for Sean Treacy? Him it was who fired the first shots of the Troubles, him and Dan Breen, and then rescued his friend Sean Hogan at the railroad station of Knocklong. Sean Hogan was taken by the Auxiliaries, and Sean Treacy took him right from the train, out from under their eyes. Tipperary boys they were, all of them, but Sean Treacy was shot down in the streets of Dublin, shot dead by the Tans, and not far from this very house, either. Do you know the song?"

"I don't think so."

"Oh, if I had half a voice I would sing it for you."

"I'd love to learn it."

"Oh, but I'm no singer. I've an agreement with the Clancy Brothers, don't you know. They don't rent out rooms and I don't sing songs, and it's a sight better for everyone that way."

"Could you teach me the song?"

"You'll be laughing at my voice."

"Oh, no, I wouldn't. Let me get my tape recorder so that I don't miss any of it. Please?"

"You wouldn't be sending me up, would you?"

"No, I mean it."

"Well..."

Ellen hurried to her room, got her tape recorder, and threaded a roll of tape onto the spool. She brought it downstairs and sat in the parlor, and the woman put down her dust cloth and perched on the edge of a massive armchair with a timid smile on her lips. She led into the old ballad gradually, talking of Sean Treacy and just where he had been killed and by whom. When she finally worked into the song itself she sang it beautifully. Her voice was thin, and she missed occasional high notes, but the tune carried sweet and clear, and the words were delivered with an air of conviction that brought the spirit of the Black and Tan days sharply into focus. The woman sang as she spoke, in a soft and gentle Dublin accent that was as far removed from the tones of the rest of Ireland as it was from the stage-Irish brogue of a Barry Fitzgerald movie.

Ellen sat very still, absorbed in the song, caught up in the dying lament of Sean Treacy for "Tipperary so far away." This was an extraordinary country, she thought, where a woman could sing for the pure joy of singing, where patriotism came from the heart rather than being summoned up perfunctorily at American Legion clambakes and Fourth of July picnics.

"That was beautiful," she said when the song had ended. "That was truly beautiful."

"Oh, now."

"I mean it."

"Ah, you must have been to Blarney Castle on your way

to Dublin. And listen to me singing with a whole house to clean! But if it's songs you want, you'll find them in Ireland. Though there's few who'll sing them as sweetly as you."

Back in her room, Ellen put the tape recorder away, then took up the guitar for a moment and picked out the melody line of "Sean Treacy." She would learn the words later, from the tape. It wasn't a song she expected to sing often. It was more a man's song and less the sort of thing she could put over effectively, and she did not expect to record it. But she might sing it now and then in concert, and she would certainly enjoy learning it and singing it herself.

Reluctantly, she returned the guitar to the case and walked down the stairs and out of the house. It was still raining, but not heavily enough to make her want her raincoat. She walked on Amiens Street as far as Talbot Street, then turned right and walked half a block to a small café. She had fish and chips and a pot of strong tea. The fish was whiting, very fresh and fried to a turn. She finished it all and drank two cups of tea, and when she left the café the sun was shining and the rain had halted.

She spent the afternoon walking until her feet ached. She began on O'Connell Street, the main artery of Dublin, and stood for a moment in front of the General Post Office where Padraig Pearse proclaimed the Irish Republic on Easter Monday in 1916. She walked on, past old hotels and new office buildings, airline ticket offices and travel bureaus, shops and cinemas and restaurants. She paused in the middle of the O'Connell Street Bridge—the bridge was wider than it was long—and watched the gulls sweeping over the Liffey. She walked on the quays along the southern bank of the Liffey, looked in the windows of antique shops, passed workmen's

pubs where laborers sat with their pints of stout. She found
Christ Church Cathedral, thinking at first that it was where
Jonathan Swift had presided for so many years, then remembering that he had been Dean of St. Patrick's instead. But
she entered the cathedral anyway and stood at the tomb of
Strongbow, the Norman earl who had led the first English
invasion of Ireland in the twelfth century.

The cathedral was empty. She stood quite alone by Strongbow's tomb and looked from it to the altar and back again.
Not even in London, at the Tower or at the Abbey, had she
felt herself so forcibly gripped by the presence of History. The
bones of great men, she thought.

She walked for hours. Now and again it would begin
raining. Then the rain would cease, only to resume again
before long. She walked on through it, oblivious to it. She
had bought a small tourist's map of Dublin, and from time
to time she would dig it out of her purse and try to figure
out where she was and what landmark she could search out
next. But each time she quickly let herself get lost, wandering
down whatever old street appealed to her, trying to immerse
herself entirely in the city. It was as though she were trying to
swallow the city whole, to gulp it all down at once and digest
it at her leisure.

She passed St. Stephen's Green and the fine shops on
Dawson and Molesworth Streets. She walked through the
gates and onto the campus of Trinity College. She passed a
few minutes in the Long Room of the library, saw the busts
of a hundred great men, glanced hurriedly at *The Book of Kells*
and other ancient illuminated manuscripts, magnificently detailed volumes dating from the eighth and ninth centuries.
Christianity had come to Ireland long before it took root in

the rest of the British Isles, and with its coming the Irish had grown as a nation of saints and scholars, missionaries to the whole of Europe. She thought of St. Patrick and St. Columba and of the song that boasted the Irish claim to a civilization older than England's.

> *And Patrick taught us gospels, and good Columba too*
> *While you threw rocks and climbed tall trees and*
> *painted your bottoms blue . . .*

Her feet refused to carry her all the way back to The White House. She got as far as the bridge over the Liffey and gave up, hailing a taxi and sinking gratefully into her seat. Back in her room, she drew the curtains shut and stretched out on the soft bed. She had stopped at the Abbey Theatre for a ticket for the evening performance and didn't know if she would have the strength to go. Maybe a nap would help; if necessary, she could skip dinner and get something to eat after the show.

She set her alarm clock for seven-thirty, kicked off her shoes, and settled her head on her pillow. She was asleep before she knew it, and she slept quite without moving until the alarm sounded.

The Abbey Theatre had just recently reopened in new quarters on the original Abbey Street site. Fifteen years earlier the building had burned to the ground, and the players had undergone a long period of exile in the old Queen's Theatre. Now, in the impressive modern building, Ellen sat watching a performance of Sean O'Casey's *The Plough and the Stars*.

The play had had its premiere at the Abbey, and she read in the theater program how an early audience had rioted over the scene in which the Republican flag was carried into a pub, seeing the scene as an insult to Ireland.

She looked at the crowd around her. Many members of the audience were tourists like herself who wouldn't think of visiting Dublin without spending a night at the historic theater. But many of the others were just as obviously native Dubliners who still drew excitement from the city's traditional drama. There would be no riots now, she knew; the play had become accepted as a classic of the Irish stage, and it was impossible to imagine anyone's becoming incensed by it.

She sat absorbed in the drama of the Easter Rising as reflected in the lives of a handful of Dublin slum dwellers. O'Casey's characters lent a deeply human touch to the harsh facts of the rebellion. And her thoughts went to the streets through which she had passed that afternoon, the buildings she had seen that had played out their parts in the Rising. The Post Office on O'Connell Street, where Pearse proclaimed the Republic and where he and a handful of men held out against the British Army for almost a week. St. Stephen's Green, where the Countess Markievicz commanded a detachment of rebels and strode through a hail of bullets, giving orders like a man. The unity of past and present in the city was overwhelming. Every stimulus touched her in a different way. The songs she had learned to sing, the history she had read, the play she watched now, the very streets of the city— all combined to give her a sense of involvement that was novel and exciting to her.

Soldiers are we
Whose lives are pledged to Ireland . . .

After the final curtain, the audience rose for "The Soldier's Song," Ireland's national anthem. Even the anthem itself was a sort of folk song, she thought, written by the rebel balladeer Peader Kearney as a marching song for the Volunteers in the days before the Rising. She left the theater hungry for more singing, hungrier for it in fact than she was for food. She had not had time to eat dinner before the play, but she decided that dinner could wait.

She walked up Abbey Street to O'Connell and hailed a taxi. "I'd like to go to a pub where there's singing," she said. "Is there a place you could take me to?"

The driver turned and studied her. "You're all alone, Miss?"

"Yes."

"American, are you?"

"That's right."

"Well, there's many pubs that have singing but not all of them that you'd care to go to by yourself. Shall I take you to O'Donoghue's? Your Ted Kennedy went there when he wanted to hear good Irish singing, and that should be recommendation enough. And it's in a decent neighborhood, such as you wouldn't mind setting foot in late at night."

"Will it be all right that I'm alone?"

"Oh, some may give you the disapproving eye, but don't pay it no mind. And as soon as they find you're American they'll take no heed of you. They'll just think that you're a bit daft to go out alone but that all Americans are a bit daft anyway, so what matter?"

Chapter 4

At first, entering the crowded, brightly lit pub, she thought she had made a mistake. There was no singing, and indeed no singing could have been heard over the hubbub of dozens of young men all talking at once. Men were lined up four deep at the bar, drinking whiskey from stemmed glasses or beer or stout from heavy glass mugs. She stood uncertain for a moment until a waiter came to her and told her there were no tables presently available.

"I thought there was singing," she said. "Will it start later, or don't you have it any more?"

"Oh, you've come for the singing." He smiled. "You'll find it upstairs in the lounge, Miss. Do you see, you've come in the bar entrance, and the lounge has a separate entrance over to the side. Come, I'll show you."

He led her out to the street again and a few yards to the right, where a door opened onto a flight of steep stairs leading up to the lounge. When he opened the door she heard the sounds of singing. "Now you just follow your ears, and if it's singing you're after, you'll find your fill up there."

At the head of the stairs she opened another door and stepped into a small, softly lighted room. A circular bar stood in the center of it, and within the bar a very thin young man with carrot-colored hair and a great beak of a nose sat at a piano. There were just a few empty stools at the bar, and four of the six tables at the sides were occupied. She started toward a table, then changed her mind abruptly and took a seat at the bar. The pianist was playing "The Boys from Wexford" and singing out the lyrics in a rich baritone, and the audience was joining in on the chorus.

"Your pleasure, Miss?"

She looked up into the broad, ruddy face of the bartender. She had come for the singing, and it had somehow failed to occur to her that she would have to have something to drink. She didn't know what to order. She liked wine, but no one else seemed to be drinking it. The men at the bar—she was the only woman there, although there were women at the tables—all seemed to be drinking beer or stout.

"Stout, please," she said.

"A pint of Guinness?"

"Please."

He held a pint mug under the tap and filled it to overflowing with the thick black stout. She put a ten-shilling note on the bar, and he gave her three half crowns in change. She took a tentative sip of the stout and wrinkled her lip at the taste. It was quite a bit warmer than American beer and very lightly carbonated. It was very strong and very bitter, and she didn't think she much cared for it. But perhaps one had to acquire a taste for it, like oysters or olives—though in fact she had never managed to develop much enthusiasm for either.

She took another sip of the Guinness. Perhaps, she thought, it would get better as one got closer to the bottom of the glass. She wondered whether she ought to light a cigarette. Actually, she thought, she probably didn't belong at the bar at all, but ought to be at a table. Or perhaps she had already violated propriety merely by coming unescorted. She recalled the taximan's words— "All Americans are a bit daft." She took out a cigarette and lit it.

For almost half an hour she sat in silence, listening intently to the singing without joining in herself. She had a bit more of her stout and noticed that it did seem to taste better, though her lips still puckered at its bitterness. At least it was an effective antidote for her hunger, if not a proper substitute for a real dinner.

Mostly she watched the singer or gazed down at her hands and the pint of stout between them. Twice, though, she looked up, to catch the eye of a young man seated halfway around the bar from her. He was tall, with a broad forehead and long black hair, and when he joined in the singing his voice was one of the loudest in the room. He seemed to know the words to almost everything that was sung, although he wasn't so good when it came to melody; he frequently sang off-key and often lost the tune entirely. But this didn't bother her nearly so much as the way he seemed to keep looking at her.

She thought of girls at college who had come back from European vacations with tales of being pinched in Rome or propositioned in Florence. She had rather envied them at the time, and now she smiled at the thought of being so intently eyed herself by a handsome Irishman in a Dublin pub.

But once she began to join in the singing, her own voice soft but sure and clear in tone, she stopped noticing the tall young man on the other side of the bar. She joined with the others in calling requests to the piano player, and she was taking swallows of the rich black stout now instead of merely sipping at it, and before she knew it her glass was quite empty. It wasn't bad at all, she decided. She felt pleasantly lightheaded. She lit another cigarette and asked the barman for another pint. She took a deep drag on her cigarette and a big swallow from the fresh pint of stout and wondered if perhaps she was getting just a little bit tipsy. After all, she hadn't had anything to eat since just past noon, so she was drinking on an empty stomach. And how strong was stout, anyway? It ought to be like beer, but then it *tasted* much stronger than beer . . .

"Sing 'The Patriot's Mother,'" she called to the pianist. "Do you know that one?"

"Just the chorus."

"Ah, that's a fine old air," another man said. "Let's hear it, Tim."

"I would, but I don't know the words. Just the chorus."

"I know the verses." She spoke without thinking. "I mean . . ."

"Then sing for us, girl."

"Oh, I couldn't. I—"

"Come, give us the song." It was the young man whose eyes she had caught. "We're none of us professionals here except Tim, and he hears so much bad singing every night that it wouldn't bother him a bit. Give us the song."

She let herself be talked into it. The song was a favorite of hers, and she had managed to put it on one of her records. It was the song of an Irish mother imploring her captured son to be true to Ireland and die on the gallows rather than turn informer. It was corny and sentimental, and once at the Gaslight on MacDougal Street she had sung it humorously, holding a shawl over her head and singing in a comic brogue, playing the old ballad for laughs. It had gone over well, but she had sung it straight on the record and she did it straight now.

Softly she began.

> *Oh, tell us the names of the rebelly crew*
> *That lifted the pike on the Curragh with you*
> *Come tell us this treason and then you'll go free*
> *Or right quickly you'll swing from the high gallows*
> *tree*

And the chorus:

> *Alanna, Alanna, the shadow of shame*
> *Has never yet fallen on one of our name*
> *And oh, may the food from my bosom you drew*
> *In your veins turn to poison if you turn untrue*

She was performing now, and she loved it. The song coursed through her veins, sang in her blood, and the music flowed from her like a river. No introduction, no round of applause, but it was a performance, and the others recognized it. At first some started to join in the chorus. Then, as if in response to a signal, their voices died out and left her to carry on alone.

> *I've no one but you in this whole world wide*
> *Yet false to your pledge you'll not stand at my side*
> *If a traitor you be you'll be farther away*
> *From my heart than if true you were wrapped in the*
> *clay*
> *Alanna, Alanna, the shadow of shame . . .*

Often, at an informal hootenanny or a Village party, she and other singers made it a practice to leave out some of the less vital verses in the longer ballads. Many of the old songs were well nigh endless, and it seemed a kindness to cut them short. One friend of hers knew over forty verses to "Stackolee," and she herself knew almost as many to "Greensleeves," and rarely sang more than five or six at a sitting.

Now, though, she did not omit a single quatrain. She sang all seven verses and sang the chorus each time, sang with her head tilted back and her eyes closed and her body perched comfortably on the bar stool, sang with the room still and silent around her, sang with the piano providing sure but restrained background accompaniment, sang with her own fingers itching for want of her guitar. She sang, and at last finished singing, and for a long moment the room was deathly still. And then there was applause, a sudden, astonishing, thunderous burst of applause. It was the first applause of the evening, and she thought that she was going to cry.

"But you're a singer, girl! Here we were playing at singing and you with a voice like that and keeping still . . ."

"Fifteen years if it's a day since a woman sang a song to make me cry, and begod if you haven't half-done it tonight . . ."

"John, give the girl a drink. Drink up, Miss, and have another. John, tell her to put her money away, it's all counterfeit and she can't spend a penny of it here. Drink up, you nightingale!"

"Not a Dublin girl, are you? And are you singing professional? Have you made any records?"

"Ah, my girl, give us another!"

She could not remember ever having felt so proud and happy. She drained her mug of stout in a swallow, and the barman filled it again for her, and there was suddenly a lump in her throat so massive that she thought she could never possibly sing through it.

She said, "Oh, if I only had my guitar . . ."

"Sean, go get the girl a guitar. Get a guitar for the lady. Don't you have one?"

"I've a banjo . . ."

"Can you play the banjo, Miss?"

"Not very well. I—"

"Then it has to be a guitar, Sean. Hasn't Jimmy Daly one? Not that he could play more than a bird call on it."

"Then wake him and tell him we need a guitar for Miss— now I don't know your name, do I?" The pianist introduced himself with a gesture. "I'm Tim Flaherty, and pleased to be of service to you, and these" —a wave at the rest of the men at the bar— "are all good lads, but you'll live as good a life without knowing them by name—"

"Ah, go on with you, Tim!"

"—but we don't know your name, Miss, and I'm sure it's one we'll want to know."

"Ellen Cameron."

"You've the voice of an angel, Miss Cameron. Will you let us have another while Sean goes for the guitar?"

"Do you know 'The Royal Blackbird,' Miss Cameron?"

"Now let her be singing what she wants," the piano player said sternly. And, sweetly now, "Come, give us a song, Miss Cameron. But first have a taste of that pint to wet your throat. A woman that can sit at a bar and drink her stout and sing with the voice of an angel and still be as sweet and pretty as spring flowers. Oh, I'd marry you in a minute, Miss Cameron, but what would my good wife say to that, do you suppose?"

She had never felt so grand and fine in all her life. Now and then in her daydreams she had imagined herself successful and had tried to guess how she might feel at such moments. Onstage at Carnegie Hall, with the audience on their feet applauding. Or during a guest appearance on a television show, singing at a camera and knowing she was being seen and heard by millions upon millions of people. She had tried to imagine these feelings, and yet nothing her imagination had summoned up could equal the way she felt now, snug in the upstairs lounge of a Dublin pub, just pleasantly tipsy on fine, rich stout (and the bitter taste had miraculously ceased to bother her by now; she rather fancied it) and singing to a group of excited and responsive persons who hung on to every word and every note.

She wanted to speak but did not trust herself to talk, certain that she would stammer or cry or both. Her emotions were too strong. She could not get hold of them. So instead of talking she tilted her head like a bird and sang like a bird greeting the dawn.

She sang on into the night, song after song after song. She urged the others to trade songs with her, but they refused. Now and then she persuaded them to join in on a chorus, but most of the time she was the performer and they were the delighted audience, and the evening took on a special magic for her. She sang songs from her albums and songs she had not yet recorded, Irish songs and Scottish songs and English and American songs, and when Sean came back with the guitar she seized it gratefully with eager hands and did a quick job of tuning it and began to play. It was a cheap guitar, with none of the resonance of her own instrument, and ordinarily she would have been put off by its poor tonal quality. Now it did not matter. Her fingers plucked at the strings and her throat opened in song and she thought that she could sing forever, that the night could go on for a thousand years and she would never tire of it.

She did not even notice when the last round was called. But the overhead lights went on just as she came to the end of a song, and she saw that the others had got to their feet.

"Oh," she said.

The barman said, "Closing time, Miss Cameron. A few minutes past, to be truthful, but the last song was worth bending the rules for. Though I wish we could stay open all night."

"Oh," she said. She got up from her stool. The music was gone now and the room started to go around in lazy waves.

"You can finish your pint, though, Miss Cameron."

"Oh," she said again, stupidly. She reached for her glass, and the room went around again, and she set the glass down untasted. Her hands gripped the bar for support and it seemed to sway before her as if it were made of elastic. "Oh, I don't think I better," she said. "Oh . . ."

"Are you all right now, Miss Cameron? Someone see to her. Miss Cameron—"

"I think it's just that the last pint was more than she wanted, John," a voice said. "She'll be fit in a minute. Come this way, Miss Cameron, and have a seat for a moment." Strong, gentle hands took her by the shoulders and led her to a chair at the side of the room. She sat down but the room kept making its lazy circles. *Sit and talk and watch a hawk making lazy circles in the sky.* But it wasn't a hawk, it was a room, and oh, she felt so funny, and—

"Are you all right now?"

She looked up into the face of the man who had been gazing across the bar at her earlier in the evening. He held her wrists gently, and his eyes met hers. "How do you feel? Not sick, are you?"

"Noooo, I'm not sick." She peered owlishly at him. "I think," she said very seriously, "that I think I drank I think too much. Stout. Too much stout."

She heard an odd sound, like the tinkling of many bells, and then realized with a start that it was her own laughter she heard. *Oh, this is so silly!* she thought, and she said, "Oh, this is so silllllly!" and exploded into laughter again.

"I'd better get you out into the fresh air," he said.

"Okay."

"Some air will be good for you."

"Okay."

He straightened up and helped her to her feet. She maintained her balance for a moment, then sagged helplessly against him. "This is so silly," she said. "Oh, wait a minute, we forgot the guitar."

"Sean took it."

"Who's Sean?"

"The boy who brought the guitar."

"Oh, that's right. I think I remember now. I learned a song today about Sean Treacy, except I didn't learn it yet. It's on the tape recorder. On tape. Scotch tape. Irish tape. It's on my Irish tape recorder. When Irish tape recorders are smiling. I don't know you, sir."

"I'm David Clare."

"That's where the priest came from. Clare, I mean. County Clare. Imagine if he came from County David. You were looking at me before. I saw you."

"Oh, was I?"

"Uh-huh. Oh, goodness, I'm sure there weren't so many steps on the way up. You won't let me fall, will you?"

"No."

"Mr. County David Clare will protect me from falling. Good evening, Mr. Clare, I'm Ellen Cameron. I'm Miss Cameron and I have the voice of an angel nightingale. I didn't even like that stout when I first tried it, but with you looking at me I couldn't just sit there, I had to do something. Imagine if I liked it. Oh, it's raining again. It always rains. It's the most wonderful city in the world but it always rains."

He was laughing. "I think we'd best walk a bit, and then get you something to eat."

"I didn't have dinner."

"You didn't?"

"No. There wasn't time." She walked at his side, breathed deeply, filling her lungs with the fresh, moist air. Her head was clearer now. "I went to the Abbey, and I was going to have dinner afterward but I came here instead."

"You must be starving."

She hadn't been until he mentioned it, but now she was.

"No wonder the stout made such an impression on you. You were drinking on an empty stomach. Have you had stout before?"

"No."

"Did you like it?"

"Not at first."

"It grows on you, doesn't it? There's a café on the next block that should still be open. We'll get you a couple of lamb chops and some potatoes."

"And no stout," she said.

They were alone in the café except for the sleepy-eyed

waitress and an old man who sat reading the *Irish Press* and nursing a cup of tepid tea. She had two lamb chops and two rashers of bacon and a plateful of chips and a cup of fairly good coffee. The food helped. When they left she was still lightheaded, but her stomach had settled down and the world no longer dipped and swayed before her eyes. She felt grand but very tired, and he read her mind to say, "I'd better get you home. Where are you staying?"

"The White House. It's on Amiens Street—in Amiens Street, I mean. That's how you say it here, isn't it? Are you from County Clare, sir? Or are you a Dublin lad? Am I a Dublin girl?" She held his arm and peered up at him. "I think," she said, "that the stout hasn't entirely worn off."

"I suspect you're right."

"But you didn't tell me. Are you from Dublin?"

He hailed a taxi, helped her into it, and took a seat beside her. He gave the driver her address and lit two cigarettes, passing one of them to her. "Sure, and can't you tell me birthplace by me brogue? And isn't it in the pure tones of the west that you hear me speaking to ye?"

"What part of the west?"

"County Galway it is," he said, "and the little town of Ballyglunnin that's me birthplace, and doesn't me sainted mother live there to this day. And doesn't she every day wrap her shawleen about her and go to the ould bog to cut turf for the fire, for to take the damp from her poor ould bones."

He went on, and she thought that his brogue had not been nearly so strong before, or perhaps she hadn't noticed it, but now it was hard to understand him, and some of the words he spoke were not ones that she knew. And then, as the taxi turned on Amiens Street just a block from her hotel, she looked at him and caught the light in his eyes and the way his lip was struggling to keep from curling in a grin.

"You," she said carefully, "are putting me on."

"Sure, and ye've found me out."

"You're not from County Galway at all."

"Sure, and where's the harm to a body if a lad has a bit of innocent sport with a pretty—"

"You're not even Irish."

He grinned at her. "Well, that's not entirely true," he said, speaking all at once in an accent straight from the Eastern Seaboard. "My father's Philadelphia Irish. Blood will tell, you know."

"You fooled me."

"I can put on a fair brogue. I've been here long enough."

"If I were entirely sober," she said, "you wouldn't have fooled me."

The taxi drew up in front of The White House. "This," David Clare said, "is where you get off. And this is where I pick you up tomorrow morning. How's ten o'clock?"

"But . . . I don't—"

"And hurry inside and get to bed. It's raining, in case you hadn't noticed."

"But who *are* you? I don't understand. I—"

"Ten o'clock," he said. "Wear comfortable shoes. I will come prepared to Tell All. Good night, Ellen Cameron."

He spoke to the driver, and the taxi moved away from the curb. She stood for a moment watching it until it turned a corner and disappeared from view.

Chapter 5

He was as good as his word. At ten o'clock, as she sat in her room studying her map of the city, basking in the afterglow of a deep sleep and a lavish breakfast, there was a knock on her door.

"A gentleman to see you, Miss Cameron. He's waiting in the parlor for you."

She had not truly expected him to come. She went downstairs, and he got to his feet and crossed the room to meet her. He held a cloth cap in both hands and stood before her with his head lowered like a servant.

"Your personal guide ready to show you all of Dublin, mum," he said. "But sad to say me limousine's broke down, and it's on foot that we'll be after walkin'."

They walked all over the city, and by noon she was certain she would need to buy a new pair of shoes before she left Dublin. He took her to some of the places she had seen the day before, but he showed them to her in a new light. They walked through Trinity College together, where he was pursuing a master's degree in history.

"Pursuing it at a leisurely pace," he added. "I've been here two years already, and it'll be another year before I finish my thesis."

"Does it usually take that long?"

"No," he admitted. "But I'm in no hurry to get the degree itself. It's just a piece of paper, when you come right down to it, and I'm more interested in learning the things I want to learn than in getting my studies finished. I'm on a teaching fellowship, and living's cheap over here, so money's not a problem."

He took her once again through the Long Room of the library. Before, the old manuscripts had been breathtaking; now, with his knowledge and enthusiasm bringing them to life for her, they took on far greater fascination. Together they bent over a gleaming glass case to examine a page of *The Book of Armagh,* written by the monk Ferdomnach in the early ninth century. "The man spent a lifetime copying this manuscript," he told her. "It's hard to imagine such an investment of time in an age when we run off a million copies of a book in a matter of days. But how many of us manage to spend our lives creating anything as important as this?"

Later, as they left the college and walked past the building that had housed Ireland's first parliament, he talked more about himself. He had just finished his summer courses, he explained, and would not be attending classes again until January. His advisor had approved a leave of absence until then, and he planned to spend the time learning the Irish language.

"Do you have to know it for your research?"

"Well, it certainly won't hurt," he said, "but I'm sure I could get along well enough without it. If my particular area of study were the old Celtic times, then a knowledge of Irish might be necessary. But most of the records of the Rebellion of Ninety-eight are in English, or else available in English translation."

"Is that your subject?"

He nodded. "It's a funny thing about Irish history. It's nothing but a record of unsuccessful rebellions from the Norman invasion clear up to the present century. The British kept planting the country with fresh settlers, and within a generation the new arrivals became Irish and rose up against England. The Rebellion of 1798 was the rising that struck the most responsive chord with me, and so I decided to go into it in more detail. You probably know some of the songs that came out of it."

"A few. Not as many as I'd like to know."

"I could teach you some, if only I could sing decently."

"Oh, will you?"

"You know what my voice is like."

"Don't be silly."

"Don't you be silly. I can't carry a tune in a wheelbarrow."

"That doesn't matter."

They walked on, and he talked about his plans to learn the language. "They have classes in Irish. They've been trying to encourage study of the old language since the turn of the century, but not too many of the young people have much enthusiasm for it. But I won't be going to classes."

Instead, he explained, he would be spending the next few months far in the west of Ireland, in the Connemara region of County Galway. This was one of the areas that comprised the Gaeltacht, the general name for regions where the original Gaelic tongue was still spoken by the inhabitants as the language of everyday life. By living among the people, by meeting with them in the markets and at the pubs, he hoped to learn Irish as a spoken, living language, not as one would learn Latin or classical Greek.

"But will you be able to retain the language when you go back to America?"

"I'm not sure that I will go back."

"You mean you'd stay here?"

"Why not?" He spread his arms wide, a gesture that took in the whole of Dublin and the surrounding country as well. "Why would anyone want to leave this place? Yesterday you saw it in the rain, and now you're seeing it in the sunshine. Either way it's the sweetest spot in the world. The people know how to live here. No one's in a hurry, no one bustles about in a mad rush to join the Coronary Club by his fortieth birthday. Life is lived at its own pace."

"But could you really feel at home here?"

"I already do," he said. "Don't you?"

"I'm not sure . . ."

"Look," he said. "I'm an historian. In America an historian is someone who spends his life on a college campus teaching dull little freshmen what happened in eighteen fifteen. And publishing deadly articles in professional journals that nobody reads. And making a rotten living in the bargain. If I stay here I can spend my time doing nothing but research and writing. The cost of living is so much lower here that a man can make a comfortable living by writing an occasional book for the American market. And I'd be close to my sources here. Remember, Ellen, Irish history is my field. It's one thing to study Michael Dwyer in the domed library of the University of Eastern Idaho or some such place. It's another thing entirely to pack a knapsack and take a walk in the Wicklow hills where Dwyer and his men made their camp. It makes the whole thing come to life."

This, she thought, was certainly something she could

understand. Just as the actual feel of a place transformed old books and documents into living history for him, the physical presence of Ireland made the old songs into much more than words and music in her own eyes.

Did she herself feel at home in Ireland? She had told him that she was not sure, and now she asked herself the question again. She did not feel like a native, certainly, but neither did she feel like a stranger. And she thought of those hours spent at O'Donoghue's the night before, perched on a stool with a borrowed guitar in her hands and a pint of stout on the bar before her and the world's most truly appreciative audience hanging on every note she sang . . .

That night he took her to the Irish Cabaret at Jury's, an old hotel in the heart of the city. They sat at a table down front and ate Irish stew and shared a bottle of French wine.

"The show's strictly for tourists, of course," he told her. "Most of the songs you'll hear aren't true Irish songs at all. They're what Dubliners call *Oirish*. Sentimental numbers like 'Galway Bay' and 'Mother Machree' and all. They became popular with homesick Irishmen in America, and of course, the American tourists expect to hear them when they come back to the ould sod. But they do a good job here, and I think you'll enjoy it. There's a chorus of young girls who sing beautifully."

She sat entranced throughout the show. Even the ventriloquist with his stage-Irish dummy delighted her, and the little girls, all of them around ten or eleven years old, were an unadulterated joy with their songs and dances. They were all quite beautiful with their long black hair and pink cheeks and bright blue eyes, and it was worth the price of the evening just to look at them.

They walked home from Jury's. The rain had still held off. "Think of it," he said, "a whole day without a drop of rain. Hard to believe we're really in Dublin." The night was glorious, cool but not chilly, the air clear and gloriously fresh and sweet in her lungs.

"I'll call for you tomorrow," he said at her door. "Is ten a good time for you?"

"Oh, you don't have to—"

"But I want to."

"I hate to take up your time. I know you have other things you have to do, and—"

"I'm all finished with classes for the summer—remember? And my time's my own until I get on the bus for Connemara. Until then I'm a gentleman of leisure, and I can't think of a way I'd rather spend my leisure than with such a lovely young lady."

"Oh, get off with your blarney and don't be after turning a poor girl's head!"

"Why, you're learning the language, Ellen!" He smiled. "Ten o'clock?"

"Will you sing some of those songs for me? And let me tape them?"

"You drive a hard bargain, but I accept."

"Ten o'clock."

His hands found her shoulders, and she closed her eyes and waited for his kiss, but he did not kiss her. She went upstairs to her room and lay in bed thinking of him. *Don't be a fool,* she told herself. *He's good company and an excellent guide,*

and after all this time he's probably lonesome for an American
girl. But he's not in love with you, or you with him.

She told herself this and made herself believe it, or
thought she did. But all night long she tossed and turned
in her sleep, and when she awoke in the morning she knew
she had dreamed the night through, and that the dreams had
been of David Clare.

She had three more days in Dublin, and she passed almost
all her time with David. They spent a morning in the parlor
of her hotel while he sang songs into her tape recorder. His
voice was as poor as he had alleged it to be, but he came close
enough to the melody so that she wound up with a fair idea
of how the songs were supposed to sound. And, more important, he knew the full background of each of the songs he sang,
the battles they commemorated, the lives of the heroes, the
roles each had played in Ireland's fight for freedom.

He told her of Father John Murphy, the rebel priest of
Boulavogue who rallied Wexford around him, only to be exe-
cuted by the British after the final defeat at Vinegar Hill. And
he sang four ballads about Murphy.

> *God grant you glory, brave Father Murphy*
> *And open heaven to all your men*
> *The cause that called you may call tomorrow*
> *In another charge for the Green again*

In the afternoons he took her out to show her more of
the city. The botanical gardens and the President's Mansion.

The Four Courts, where the 1916 insurgents held out against British guns and where, just a few years later, Michael Collins turned the new Free State's guns upon the anti-Treaty forces of the Irish Republican Army. "No one likes to talk about the Civil War," he told her. "It's the country's shame. So many successful uprisings end that way, with the Revolution devouring her own children. Michael Collins and Arthur Griffith accepted the Treaty and the Free State. De Valera and Cathal Brugha and others rejected it. And so old comrades fought each other. Cathal Brugha died right here; he took seventeen British bullets in nineteen sixteen and lived through it, and Michael Collins's men shot him down here in nineteen twenty-two. And Collins was gunned down a few months later in an IRA ambush. The country's not all jokes and songs and poetry. There's a strain of sheer tragedy underneath it all."

One night he took her to the Abbey Tavern in Howth, a coastal suburb to the north of Dublin. He hired a car, and they drove there in the twilight. This time she brought her guitar, and although she spent most of her time listening to other singers, she did sing a few songs of her own and was as well received as the first night in O'Donoghue's. She drank enough Guinness to get just the slightest bit high, and on the way back she sat with her head on David's shoulder. When he drew to a stop at last in the still darkness of Amiens Street he took her in his arms and kissed her.

After a moment he said, "You're leaving tomorrow?"

"Yes."

"I'll miss you, Ellen."

She didn't trust herself to speak.

"You'll love the west. You may miss Dublin, but I know you'll like the rest of the country. Don't be afraid to talk to people. The only strangers in Ireland are people you haven't met. Once you meet them they stop being strangers. You should have a grand time in Tralee and Dingle. I've never been there, but I've been to other parts of County Kerry. It's beautiful country." He paused for a moment. "I know you'll do well in Berlin. And that you'll have a good trip home." Another pause. "You know, I really will miss you, Ellen."

His arms held her, and his lips found hers. She knew she was going to cry but hoped she could hold her tears until she was alone in her own room. Just a vacation romance, she told herself. He would forget her in a week, and they would never see each other again.

He walked her to her door and kissed her good night. She hurried inside without a word and rushed up the stairs and into her room. She was all prepared to cry, but now the tears refused to come.

Hardly a grand passion, she told herself. Just a very pleasant way to pass the time in Dublin.

> *And so I knew that she would do*
> *With all of the tricks I knew she knew*
> *To pass away the time in Venezuela*

Would she ever see him again? Probably not, she thought. And if she did, they would probably have blessed little to say to each other. This week had been a delicious accident, a moment when each was ready for the other.

> *I never shall marry*

And the rest of the trip would be good, she told herself fiercely. It would be exciting, and she would forget him.

I'll be no man's wife

She slipped out of her clothes and snuggled under the bedcovers. It was cold in her room. She pulled the quilts up to her chin and settled her head on her pillow.

I'm bound to stay single

Damn that song! Why did it have to run through her head this way? Why?

All the days of my life

Chapter 6

She left The White House almost immediately after breakfast. She settled her bill and carried her suitcase and guitar and tape recorder to a waiting taxi. The bus station was only a few blocks away, but it was too far for her to carry everything on foot. She had half-hoped and half-feared that David might call that morning to say a last goodbye to her, and she was both glad and sorry that he did not appear. Goodbyes had always been difficult for her, and although she would have liked to see him a final time, she was relieved that she would be spared the awkwardness of another leavetaking. He had said he would miss her, and she knew full well that she would miss him.

Her bus left at the appointed hour, though David had cautioned her to approach all Irish schedules with a certain amount of skepticism. "An Irish mile is about a fourth again as long as an English mile," he said. "I suspect the national character has something to do with it, because an Irish hour often turns out to be half a day. Just be confident that the bus will leave sooner or later and reach its destination sooner or later. Don't pay too much attention to the time. That's one of the charms of the country. You can get along very well without ever looking at a clock. Sometimes I leave my watch in my room for weeks at a time and never miss it."

But this particular bus had left on time, and she sat a few seats behind the ruddy-faced bus driver and looked out the window as the old bus left Dublin and headed south. David had helped her plan her route, although he had impressed upon her the need to keep her plans flexible. "Just remember that you want to arrive in Tralee in time for the Festival of Kerry, and let things follow their own course between now and then. The best part of a trip is slipping off your schedule and getting caught up in some fascinating surprise. I feel so sorry for the poor fools who take those carefully arranged tours. Breakfast in Paris, sightseeing for the morning, lunch in Florence, shopping in the afternoon, dinner in Rome, a tour of the nightclubs, a morning flight to Vienna—I don't know how they stand it. They might as well stay at home and watch a Technicolor travelogue at the movies. A trip should be more personal than that. It should move at its own pace. That way it can keep on surprising you—and travel's no fun without surprises."

Still, she had sat with him while they mapped out a rough itinerary. She was heading south now, through the Wicklow Mountains toward County Wexford. She would spend the night in Wexford City and then head west along the southern edge of the country. There were parts of Waterford and Tipperary that she wanted to see, along with Cork City and parts of western Cork and Kerry. The itinerary was purposefully vague, the timetable almost nonexistent. She was not sightseeing so much as she was seeking out new songs and native singers, and so she would go where the material could be found.

The first couple of days on the road, while delightful, were musically unproductive. Despite David's advice, she found it impossible to overcome her natural shyness and approach to-tal strangers. She spent the night and part of a day in Wexford City, touring churches and a small museum, spending quietly satisfying hours in a local café and breathing the fresh salt air of the seaside town. But she left her guitar in her room, and she did not hear people singing where she went.

Several times the local tradesmen spoke to her. They were excited to hear that she was an American, since tourists were more of a rarity in Wexford than in Dublin. Almost everyone she spoke to had relatives in the States and was anxious to talk about America. Often the pubs and stores sported color por-traits of Kennedy, and people seemed anxious to talk about the Irish lad who had become America's president.

But no one sang. When she told of the motive for her trip, of her desire to collect new material, everyone was interested and sympathetic and quite useless. "You'll want to go to the west," she heard more than once, "where they're a regular race of singers. We've nothing so unusual here, sad to say."

A bus took her westward from Wexford to the smaller towns within the county. Here she caught the flavor of rural Ireland, a far cry from the cosmopolitan quality of Dublin. The rude little cottages, their tall rooftop television anten-nas the sole visual reminder that they were actually a part of the electronic age. The scarcity of automobiles and the great quantity of bicycles, with old men and women riding them. The sweet, timeless sensation of a walk through the center of town and a stop in a village pub. These last were wholly unlike the Dublin pubs; they were more like small grocery stores with a single counter where liquor and beer were sold for on-premises consumption.

"We're just country folk here," a woman told her at a

boardinghouse where she found a comfortable room for just sixteen shillings, breakfast included. "Not like your Dublin jackeens, so city-wise and quick like. A young lass like yourself might find nothing to do here. There's no picture show, and no night life."

"But I like it here," she said.

"Oh, and do ye? Most of our young people are after leaving. For Dublin, and some for London or America."

That night she took her guitar with her to one of the tiny pubs. She had been thinking of David, sitting in her room and remembering the time she had spent with him, and she suddenly felt a great need to be among people, to make music and hear music. There was just one other customer in the pub, an old man in cap and long coat who sat drowsily over a glass of whiskey. The woman behind the counter was reading a newspaper and smoking a cigarette. Ellen sat in a corner of the small shop and played softly on the guitar, her fingers toying with the melody of one of the songs David had taught her. She wondered if she remembered the words. It was a song of the Wexford rising, and she thought that this was the very region where the rising had taken place almost two centuries ago. She began to sing, softly, more to herself than to the others, and before she knew it the old woman had abandoned her newspaper and the man had turned from his glass of whiskey to listen to her.

"Sure, you know the old songs of Wexford!"

"Oh, one or two . . ."

"And do you know this one?" And the old man, his face all lined and pinched with age, began to sing in an impossibly sweet tenor voice. By the end of the first verse she had caught hold of the melody and was able to accompany him on the guitar. When he finished the old woman remembered a song she had sung as a child, a sweet bit of nonsense about an old woman and her pig. And then Ellen sang another song, and the pub began to fill up with other men and women, and before she knew it the evening filled with song.

It took singing to do it, she discovered. She could have gone all over Ireland, telling everyone she met that she was hunting for songs, and everyone would have nodded knowingly and sighed sadly and explained that they were no great singers in that particular part of the country but that if she would only go north or south or west or east, if she would in short only go elsewhere to some more romantic part of the nation, then she might find what she was looking for.

Yet the moment her fingers plucked at the strings of her guitar they managed to strike a responsive chord in the men and women within hearing range. Once she had raised her own voice in song, everyone was anxious to sing, and to listen to her own singing, and then it suddenly turned out that the town was a treasure trove of words and melody.

And was it songs she was after? Why, Wexford was the very home of songs, she was speedily assured. Songs of all sorts, songs in English and songs in Irish, too. Sure, the Clancys came from Carrick in Tipperary, but weren't there singers as good throughout County Wexford? And didn't they have songs right here that the rest of Ireland had never heard, much less the rest of the world? And could she stay another night? Because there would be a hooley at Paddy Molloy's house, they'd plan it here and now, with drink enough for everyone and the best voices for five miles around sure to be there. Could she bring her tape recorder? Sure, and why

not? Now if she wanted songs, why sure and they'd teach her
songs!

From that night on the whole course of her trip was completely changed. Even before the next night's hooley she began to gather material. She spent the morning and afternoon
at a table in a café around the corner from her rooming house,
and men and women were forever coming to her table to
ask her if she knew this song or that one, and singing to her
the ones she did not know. She had her tape recorder with
her and faithfully committed each new song to tape. Many
of them, she knew, would prove worthless. Some were little
more than different words to familiar tunes. Others were col-
lections of clumsy lyrics, faithful as records of this battle or
that but musically unexciting. But in spite of the large quantity of unusable material, she did succeed in gathering many
songs that would be valuable to her.

And later on at the party, there were more songs and several singers who were good enough to deserve a place on the
album of native singers she hoped to get Folklore to issue. A
small band formed itself at the party—two banjos, a tin whis-
tle, a drum, a guitar. She kept her tape recorder running con-
stantly, and when she played the tapes back the next morning
she was delighted to discover that she had better than twenty
minutes' worth of material that could be transcribed directly,
material that could stand as the core of an eminently valuable
album of Irish music.

She left the town reluctantly the next day, sad to see the
last of it but at the same time anxious to get on with her
work. She had found the formula now and was confident
that it would serve her ideally wherever she went. Singing
was contagious in Ireland. If she went among the people with

her guitar and her songs, it would not be long before she had more new material than she could ever use.

The system worked even better than she had expected. She headed steadily westward, never going very far in a single day, purposefully seeking out the smallest, quietest towns along her route. She went to towns with names that seemed themselves to be made of music, towns like Mullennakill and Ballyduff and Furraleigh and Poulnamucky and Ballylooby. She spent long, lazy afternoons walking through the green hillside down narrow winding roads bordered by fences of piled stone.

She wondered aloud once where all the stones came from, and a farmer told her with a laugh, "We come on the stones when plowing, and the only way to be rid of them is to build fences with them. If they're part of a fence they can't be in the ground, and it's hard growing praties in stone." No mortar held the stones in place. They were piled neatly one upon another, and often she came upon breaks in the fences where sheep or goats had knocked some of the stones free.

The animals seemed to wander freely, in the road as often as not. She came upon every sort of animal in the narrow roadways, sheep bleating mournfully, fat Irish cattle grazing at the roadside, plump pigs rooting in the fields, goats knocking about in pairs, their forelegs lashed together. "The sheep will usually stay where they belong," a man had told her, "but there's no holding the goats, they've always a mind to be wandering where they shouldn't be. But there's no beast less apt to cooperate than a goat, and so we tie two of them together, and then they're less quick to get over a fence. Because when one wants to go wandering the other wants to stay behind, and when that one changes his mind so does the other, and they can never quite get together, and so they stay where they're meant to stay."

Further west, in the inland plains of Tipperary, the soil was less rocky. There were fewer of the stone fences, and instead the roads were edged with massive banks of earth, the grass growing on the earthen dykes as well as it grew everywhere else in Ireland. Walking between those banks—they called them *ditches* there, a source of confusion at first because she had always thought of a ditch as a hole in the ground rather than a mound rising above ground level—walking between them, she could picture graphically the ambushes and battles of the Black-and-Tan war. She could imagine the men of the IRA flying columns crouching in the fields behind the ditches, while the Tans and Auxiliaries drove down the tortured twisted roads in their Crossley vans. Then bombs would wing down on the vans, and bold men would rest their rifle barrels on the tops of the ditches and rain fire down on the troops.

> *Oh, but isn't it grand to see*
> *The Auxies and the R.I.C.*
> *The Black-and-Tans turn tail and flee*
> *Away from Barry's column*

In the County Cork an old man led her outside of the town of Macroom to the very spot where a flying column had staged one of the major battles of the Troubles. He had not been there himself, he was quick to explain, but a cousin of his had been one of Tom Barry's men and had taken a bullet in the hip that very day. And while he pointed out just where the troops had been positioned, he sang her a song commemorating the day. The last line, as it turned out, was joyously obscene—something that did not occur to the old gentleman until he had finished singing it. He blushed furiously and apologized profusely, and it was all she could do to keep from laughing aloud. She could never record that song, she thought, and could not even sing it in mixed company, but it was one she could never forget.

> But the boys of the colyum were waiting
> With rifle and powder and shot
> And the Irish Republican Army
> Made shit of the whole fucking lot

She ran out of tape before she reached Cork City. There she bought more and made a package of the reels she had filled, mailing them to herself in New York. In Cork the pace of her trip began to catch up with her, and she discovered that she was genuinely tired, exhausted physically by the endless walking and riding and singing, exhausted mentally and emotionally by the parade of experiences she had undertaken. She stayed longer than she planned in Cork, sleeping late in the mornings and leaving her guitar snug in its case throughout her stay. She contented herself with leisurely sightseeing and spent a night at the movies watching an American Western. She met a pair of honeymooners from Chicago and talked with them, the first Americans she had seen since she left Dublin and David Clare.

David. She realized that night that she had scarcely thought of him at all during the past several days. She had been too busy, rushing to experience the whole of rural Ireland, caught headlong in the legend and song of the nation. And yet he had never been far from her mind. Now she thought of him again and wondered what the trip would have been like if he had been able to accompany her.

So often she had found herself moved by one thing or an-other—the view from a particular hill, the speech of a partic-ular man or woman, the throat-catching beauty of a particu-lar sunset. And so often she had felt the lack of someone to share those beauties with. She had never been conscious of her loneliness, but looking back she could see that she had in fact been lonely. More than once she had found herself talking aloud to herself, as if in need of rendering a verbal re-action to the phenomena that moved her. It all stemmed, if not from loneliness, at least from aloneness. She recognized this now and thought of David Clare and wished she could see him again.

I never shall marry . . .

Nonsense, she told herself. She looked at the four walls of her little room and shivered. She got dressed and left the hotel and went to the pub next door for a drink.

She did not stay long at the pub. She was in no mood for drinking and in less of a mood for music or conversation, and she went only because her room was beginning to feel like a cell. She nursed one small glass of beer and smoked two cig-arettes. Her American cigarettes were long gone now, and she had been experimenting with various English and Irish brands, none of which tasted particularly good to her. She had found one brand that lit themselves; you struck the tip of the cigarette against the side of the packet and the end ignited. It had seemed at first like a marvelous idea, and she couldn't imagine why they didn't have such cigarettes available in the

States, but she found that the principle worked better in theory than in practice. Half the time the cigarette broke in the middle while she was trying to get it lit, and when lit it tasted foul anyway.

When she left the pub she got a slight shock. On her way to her hotel she caught a glimpse of a man's face in a darkened doorway, and it looked exactly like the face of the man she had seen in London. The tall man, his long, hawklike nose bisecting his long wedge of a face, his deep, hollow eyes, his cruel, thin lips. She saw the face for only a second or two, but she found herself suddenly walking very fast, and she was short of breath as she entered her hotel. She could barely wait to be up the stairs and inside her room with her door bolted.

The whole memory of the mugging in London came back at her, sending shivers through her body. She held her hands in front of her and saw that her fingers were trembling.

Ridiculous, she told herself. Of course, it was not the same man at all, and if she got a good look at him in the light, she would probably discover that this man looked nothing like the London criminal who had choked her and stolen her purse. But her reaction was at least indicative of the impression that incident had left upon her mind. She was badly shaken.

It was ridiculous, she knew. It was not uncommon for total strangers to resemble persons whom one knew. This happened to her frequently in New York—a girl glimpsed on the street would look exactly like her college roommate, and when she ran to overtake the girl she would discover that the two looked not at all alike. And just a day ago, in Cork, she had seen a man in peasant's clothing who had for a moment seemed the spitting image of the priest she had met on the plane to Dublin. The resemblance had so startled her that she had been on the point of hailing him, until she realized he could not possibly be Father Farrell. A priest did not suddenly put on an old tweed jacket and a battered cloth cap, any more than a London hoodlum turned up in the south of Ireland.

She guessed that it was all a symptom of loneliness. When one was among strangers, one looked for familiar faces and invented them when they did not exist.

She slept badly, haunted upon awakening by a formless but notably unpleasant dream. David had been in it, she knew, and Father Farrell, and her agent in New York, and the narrow-faced man from London, but just what they had all been doing in her dream was beyond recollection. She bathed and dressed and went down for breakfast, then packed her suitcase and checked out of the hotel. It was time to leave Cork, she had decided. She had to get to Tralee soon, and she did not want to spend any more time in a city that was beginning to give her unpleasant evidence of her loneliness.

Her bus carried her to Bantry and Glengarrif, then north to Kenmare in County Kerry. She had bought a ticket straight through to Killarney, but in Kenmare she left the bus and found a room. She spent two days making side trips through the wild hills of Kerry, where the scenery had a raw and rugged splendor that made the beauties of the rest of Ireland almost pallid in comparison. The deep green of the hillsides, the stark majesty of mountains rising boldly behind deep blue lakes, the touching simplicity of tiny white cottages with thatched roofs, all made her understand why everyone throughout the whole of Ireland had assured her how much she would like Kerry.

It was a poor county, and the years had been cruel to its people. The potato famine in the middle of the nineteenth century had devastated the countryside, reducing the population to literal starvation. Thousands had gone to their graves. Thousands more had boarded ship for America. And in the years that followed, the wars had placed new hardships upon Kerry. Some of the fiercest fighting of the Troubles and the Civil War had been waged in this county at the southwest corner of Ireland. It had always been a stronghold of Republicanism, and it boasted a record of massacres and reprisals, of homes and towns burned to the ground, of midnight ambushes and midnight arrests, of brutalities and outrages on both sides.

All that ferocious fighting, all that record of misery, seemed out of place against the backdrop of sheer physical beauty. But at the same time she could sense bitterness and old violence lurking in the magnificence of the hills and the sweet green of the valleys.

She sang some songs in the small towns of Kerry, and she learned more songs and put many of them on tape. She was moving close to a part of the Gaeltacht now, though it was far removed from Connemara, where David would go to learn Irish.

The people she met spoke in a thick brogue, and she had worlds of trouble making out what some of them were saying. But gradually she learned to follow their speech. She met many persons who spoke Gaelic as often as they spoke English, and some of them sang songs for her in that tongue. She had to budget her tape very carefully to make sure she would have enough left for Tralee and Dingle.

At last it was time, time for the festival in Tralee. She was barely looking forward to it by the time she had boarded the bus for that city. The trip so far, wholly unplanned, had been a joy. Now she was back on schedule again, with her activities quite strictly laid out and her timetable admitting little flexibility. She would be a few days in Kerry, then a few more days in Dingle, then a quick bus ride to Shannon Airport, then a plane all the way to Berlin. She hardly felt up to that last stage. Already she had bitten off more than she could chew, had swallowed more new experience than she could readily digest. The idea of taking in a whole new country was almost frightening.

She sat on the bus, guitar and suitcase and tape recorder stowed in the overhead rack, as the bus rolled on toward Tralee.

Chapter 7

Tralee was half a delight and half a nightmare and all quite different from what she had expected. Folk festivals in the main were relatively tame affairs, with the attention focused on a few hours of singing and dancing. But the Festival of Kerry turned out to be a good deal more than this. It was built around a three-day race meeting, and the men and women who had come to watch the horses would have crowded the town by themselves. Besides this there was an outdoor circus, sheep-dog trials, terrier and donkey derbies, swimming and athletic competitions, street dances, marching bands parading through the little city, and a general mood of hilarity that summoned up images of New Orleans at Mardi Gras time. The folk singing was just a small portion of the total pageantry that filled Tralee to overflowing.

Rooms were not to be found. She had arrived without a reservation, and after she had wasted some time making the rounds of the hotels and rooming houses, a student from Edinburgh suggested she try the Festival Accommodations Committee. She went to their office, and a kindly woman arranged accommodations for her in a private home not far from the center of town. She was to pay five pounds for her room for the whole of the festival and would take breakfast with the family.

The price was reasonable enough, but later she thought that she might almost have done without a room altogether, for all the time she spent in it. The city bustled endlessly. The streets were thronged with tens of thousands of visitors, and the town park had the air of a three-ring circus, with several events going on at a time from morning until late at night. Students from all parts of the British Isles had turned out in full force, many of them with knapsacks on their backs. They had reached Tralee by hitchhiking, and now they slept in the park or in fields on the edge of town, cutting their expenses to the bone and hurling themselves into the festival activity with a vengeance.

Ellen was on the go for three days. Each night she crept back to her room in the small hours of the morning, careful not to wake the family with whom she was staying, and each day she left the house just after breakfast for another furious round of festival activity. The guitar, always close at hand, kept making new acquaintances for her. It stamped her as a singer, and other singers sought her out, and she spent hours in feverish conversation, swapping songs, exchanging gossip of the world of professional folk music, and making the sort of easy friendships that emerge from such hectic meetings.

She filled all the rolls of tape she had bought in Cork, and mailed them all back to herself in New York. She sang songs around campfires on the edge of town, at a party in a house that three boys from London had leased for the season, and at the base of the 1798 monument in Denny Street near the Mall. She sang and listened and ate and drank and smoked and talked and kept going as long as the festival itself kept going, waiting with throngs in the park while the Rose of Tralee was chosen and crowned, running through the streets with the mob, caught up in a frenzy of unmotivated enthusiasm, and returning, at last, the festival over for another year, to her little room in Edward Street.

She missed breakfast the next morning. She was exhausted and could barely drag herself out of bed. It was time to go to Dingle, she thought, and she wasn't sure that she wanted to go. Maybe she had had enough of folk music and festivals for the time being. Maybe she could go directly to Shannon and spend a few days in one of the lush American-style hotels near the international airport. She could well afford it, she knew; the trip so far had cost her far less than she had anticipated, and she could easily afford the luxury of a few days of lolling in an air-conditioned room and taking long baths and sleeping the day away.

"There won't be many of us going on to Dingle," a Dublin singer named Rory had told her the day before. "They don't get a tenth the crowd that Tralee does. It's a tiny town, you know, and couldn't take a crowd if it got one. They'll have some singing and dancing, but I've had my fill of that for the time being."

She, too, had had her fill of it. Most of the singing in Dingle, she had heard, would be in Gaelic, which made it unlikely that she would be able to learn any new material. She would have been delighted to tape some Gaelic songs, but that seemed impossible now, since her tape was all gone and there did not seem to be any for sale in Tralee.

No, she decided, she wouldn't go. She was already exhausted, and the festival in Berlin would certainly be taxing. Between now and then she could use all the rest she could get. Dingle had sounded like fun when she had first planned it, but after all, it was only another little Irish town, and she had already been to a great many Irish towns, small and large, and . . .

"Will you be going on to Dingle?"

"I don't know, Mrs. Sheehy," she told her landlady. "I was thinking I might go straight to Shannon and—"

"Ah, and I wish I had the time to go myself this year! We went last year, Dan and I." The woman smiled at the memory. "The first night's the most beautiful. All of us gathered at the harbor, the whole town and all of us who'd come down for the celebration. And the Rose of Tralee, she sailed up Dingle Harbor on a barge, and they touched off fireworks to greet her. Big pretty things that lighted up the whole sky. Ah, it was a beautiful thing, I tell you, and something you'll never see elsewhere. I wish it was me that was going again."

Ellen walked to the bus station, carrying guitar and suitcase and the now useless tape recorder. Fireworks and a brass band, she thought; nothing that you couldn't find in Keokuk, Iowa, on the Fourth of July. But she couldn't brush aside the enthusiasm in Mrs. Sheehy's voice. It gave a special glow to the description of the little town.

Don't be ridiculous, she told herself. *You don't have to go. There's no point to it.*

But she knew it was a lost cause. And at the little Tralee bus station she gave up the fight in good grace and bought a ticket to Dingle. If nothing else, she thought, a little seaside village might be restful. She could take her ease there as well as she could in Shannon, and no doubt at much less expense.

And there was no getting around it—she was too responsive a traveler to force herself to take it easy. She grinned gamely as the tall, red-haired bus driver helped her up the steps of the bus and placed her luggage in the rack overhead. Already, she admitted, she was looking forward to Dingle. Already the thought of doing nothing for a few days had lost its charm. The luxury hotels of Shannon would be wasted on her, so she prepared to enjoy whatever was in store for her.

The thirty-mile trip from Tralee to Dingle led through some of the most beautiful scenery in Ireland. The bus moved at a deliberate pace, stopping three times along the way at the little towns of Blennerville, Camp, and Aunascaul. On the first leg of the journey she had her choice between two equally splendid views. To her left were the Slieve Mish Mountains, their rough peaks shimmering in the sunlight. On the right Tralee Bay lay before her, soft and gloriously blue, with the "lonely Banna Strand," celebrated in so many songs, stretching out beyond the scope of her vision. Sir Roger Casement had been captured there in April 1916, taken prisoner after an attempt to persuade the Germans to provide guns and troops for an Irish rising, then spirited off to England, tried, and hanged as a traitor to the Crown.

The bus swung to the south at Camp, and before long she could see the waters of Dingle Bay on the left. The roads were circuitous now, steep and winding, with other cars appearing magically as they came around turns, and with an astonishing quantity of all sorts of animals turning up in the middle of the road. Sheep, pigs, even a pair of tethered goats, their presence giving the lie to the theory that goats would not cooperate long enough to clear a fence together. The bus moved onward, slowly but surely, somehow avoiding an accident with any of the odd creatures that cropped up in its path.

The roads were thronged, too, by another breed entirely, pilgrims bound for Dingle town. She looked out the window to see college students with packs on their backs, some walking with determination, others standing at the side of the road, their thumbs out in the universal gesture of the hitchhiker. Even if only a small percentage of the crowd from Tralee found its way to Dingle, the little village would be hard put to house the crowd. It was still early in the day, and every time the bus passed hikers and hitchhikers she had the selfish thought that she would at least beat these people in the search for a room.

"Dingle town," called the driver. She looked out the front window and saw nothing resembling a town. Then the bus curved around yet another turn in the road, and she saw the little village laid out before her at the base of the hill.

Her worries about finding a room turned out to be groundless. The first bed-and-breakfast house she tried was full, but the gentle-voiced proprietress recommended the house two doors further down on Strand Street, the main commercial street of Dingle. There Ellen found several rooms available and took a large one on the second floor just down the hall from the bathroom. She signed the register, then went to her room to unpack. On her way out of the house an older woman smiled to her and asked her if she was a folk singer.

"Why, yes, I am," she said, surprised. "How did you know?"

"Not much in the way of detective work, I'm afraid." The woman spoke in an accent Ellen had trouble placing—not

Irish, certainly, but quite unlike the English and Scottish speech she had heard. "I'm staying here myself, and I was upstairs when you checked in. Saw you had a guitar, and it seemed an odd thing to carry for decoration, so I had to assume you played it. Will you be engaging in the competition?"

"No, I haven't registered."

"The actual competition's all in Irish, I understand, though I trust there will be some songs in English. I certainly hope there will. I don't understand Irish, do you?"

"No."

"Though the sound of it is not unfamiliar. They still speak Cornish in my part of the world, and it's another of the old Celtic tongues. I wonder if the Irish speakers can understand Cornish. Probably not, I suppose; the way these languages form dialects of their own over the centuries, you know. Oh, I'm sorry, I haven't introduced myself yet, have I? I'm Sara Trevelyan, from Cornwall. The usual British schoolteacher on vacation, I'm afraid. Retired and husbandless and unutterably dull. And don't rush to tell me that I can't possibly be dull."

"I'm Ellen Cameron."

"Yes, I know." Sara Trevelyan smiled. "And from New York, aren't you? Again, no great shakes as a detective. I looked in the guest register. There's a countryman of yours who signed in just after you, incidentally. Has a German name, if I remember correctly. Now what was it?" She wrinkled her brow in thought. "Koenig," she said. "Doctor Robert Koenig, I think it was, and he's from Philadelphia, which makes you almost neighbors, doesn't it? Has a wife and two children with him. Not the most adorable children in the world, I wouldn't say, but then perhaps I'm biased against children. Taught too many of them over the years and had none of my own, and that can rather set one against children. Not that I don't admit the necessity of children, of course. You can't produce people without having children as the first stage of the game."

Ellen laughed.

"Well, it's true, isn't it? Just as you need caterpillars in order to have butterflies. Sometimes I think the parallel is a very close one at that. Horrid crawling things those caterpillars are, and look at the lovely, fragile creatures they become. And when I think of some of the dreary lads and lasses I taught over the years, and of their metamorphosis into rather worthwhile gentlemen and ladies, it's hard to believe they're all of the same species." The Cornish woman sighed. "But I do run off at the mouth, don't I? Perhaps I'm a little grateful to have someone to talk with. Are you anxious to get free of me? Or would you take lunch with an old woman if she promises not to talk too much?"

"I'd be delighted."

"I've been here since last night. Came straight from Killarney. I suppose you were in Tralee?"

"Yes."

"Crowded, was it?"

"Very much so. And very active."

"Then I'm just as glad I missed it. I'm not that strong for crowds and fast-paced holidays. I'll be glad for a chance to hear the singing, but I can hear it as well without all that hullabaloo going on. That's what you call it in America, isn't it? Hullabaloo?"

"That's right."

"But you're smiling, so I suppose I misused the colloquialism slightly, as one is apt to do. Hmmm. I was here last night, as I said. There's a restaurant just a block from here, not fancy but rather pleasant. They do grilled meats well enough. Would you like to go there? And then I'll promise to leave you alone for the rest of the afternoon."

"But I'm enjoying this very much!"

"Are you? I know that I am. I find children charmless, but I do enjoy young people. I hope you like the restaurant."

She did like the restaurant, a narrow café where a pert and pretty young waitress brought them small filet steaks and chips. And she did enjoy the company of the older woman. Cornwall, that little peninsula at the southwest corner of England, was another of the places she had long wanted to visit. She tried to remember if anyone had ever recorded an album of Cornish songs. She couldn't think of any, although it was certain that the Cornishmen would have folk music of their own, just as every little pocket of culture throughout the world did. Later, perhaps, she might ask Miss Trevelyan if she knew any of the old songs. A shame she was out of tape, but perhaps she could learn a song or two.

After lunch they parted company. The retired schoolteacher planned a hike along the beach in search of shells and a taste of salt air. She walked back to the B-and-B with Ellen and got her walking stick from her room. It was a knobby blackthorn stick, and she showed it to Ellen.

"Quite the thing, isn't it? Do you think it goes well with the tweed suit? And does it make me look properly Irish?"

"Oh, very Irish."

"I suspect it stamps me as a tourist, actually. In a week I haven't seen a single Irishman carrying one of these silly things. A great knobby stick, isn't it? I'm sure they'd never make them at all but to sell them to the English and Americans, and fools we are to buy them. Would you believe I paid four pounds for this one? And it's only a silly piece of wood."

"It's attractive, though."

"Perhaps. I do know it's a great help in walking. Well, thank you again for lunching with me. I hope we'll see each other again. You'll be in Dingle a few days?"

"Yes."

"Then I'll see you at the breakfast table, and perhaps around the town as well."

She spent the afternoon wandering around the town but not making as strenuous a project of it as the elderly Cornish lady. She window shopped at the little stores on Strand Street, wandered through the side streets among the little rows of neat well-scrubbed cottages. She stopped in a Catholic church, covering her head with a handkerchief and walking slowly through the aisles, studying the stained-glass windows and sitting for a moment before the altar. A person could find a special sort of contentment in any house of worship, a nonverbal sense of the presence of some greater force. Sitting there, in a small church in a small town deep in the southwest corner of Ireland, she thought for a moment that she would like to pray, to give thanks for the pure delight of the trip. But she had never found prayer natural, and after a few moments she got to her feet and left.

In the corridor outside her own room, she saw a round-faced, balding man shepherding a woman and two children into another room, then turning and heading for the staircase. The doctor from Philadelphia, she thought at once, and there was something strikingly familiar about him, though she could not say what it was.

"Dr. Koenig?"

He spun around, genuinely startled, when she spoke his name.

"Yes?"

"I'm sorry," she said. "I just . . . we haven't met, but I can't help feeling that I've seen you before."

"It is possible," he said stiffly. His voice had a slight trace of a German accent.

"Were you in Tralee?"

"No. No, we came direct from Dublin."

"Perhaps I saw you there."

"Perhaps," he said. "Although this is a common phenomenon, you know. The recognition of strangers. In my business, I am a psychiatrist, we have observed—"

"I hope you don't mean that I'm unbalanced?"

"Not at all." She had meant to make light of it, but the psychiatrist seemed to be a totally humorless man. "And it is possible that we have seen each other after all. I am from Philadelphia. Is that by any chance your own hometown?"

"No, but I have been there. I'm from New York."

"And I have often been to New York. Perhaps we have met on the underground. The subway, that is. One sees so many people. It is possible."

"Yes, but I just—"

"You must excuse me," he said. "My wife has found an errand for me. I hope you enjoy Dingle, Miss Cameron."

It never occurred to her to wonder how he had known her name.

*   *   *

Shortly before dinner, the rains came. It was an on-again, off-again sort of rain, a drizzling mist that let up intermittently, only to resume again before very long. It was, in short, a typically Irish sort of rain, and she knew better than to resent it. The Tralee festival had been mercifully short of rain, with the skies surprisingly clear for long stretches at a time. Now Dingle was due for a downpour, and she could hardly object to it.

"Horrid weather," Sara Trevelyan said. They sat together in the parlor downstairs, waiting for the rain to let up so that they could go around the corner for dinner. "It's a pity, really. If they could only do something about the cursed rain this area would be a veritable paradise. The summers never get too hot and the winters rarely get very cold. But it rains all the time."

"Did you get caught in it this afternoon?"

"I just got back in time."

"Did you have much luck finding shells?"

"I got a bag of them, but I'm afraid I can't tell you what they are. I'm not one of these passionate shellers who go into spasms over a one-eyed limpet or a double-breasted cowrie, I'm afraid. Never can tell one shell from the next. I just pick the pretty ones and set them out around my house. Very much the amateur, I fear."

"You probably have more fun that way."

"Perhaps."

She went to the door. "It seems to have let up a little," she said. "Shall we risk it?"

"I think not, for my part. I catch colds rather easily, and my doctor is convinced that I'll catch one and die of it if I'm not careful. I offered to bet that he'd die before me, but he pointed out it would be a difficult wager to collect, no matter who won it. An unanswerable argument. You go ahead and have your dinner, Ellen. I'll lie down for a few minutes."

"Shall I bring you back something?"

"Oh, don't bother. I'm not that hungry, actually. I'll go out later."

It was still raining after dinner, coming down a bit harder than before. She hurried from the café to the doorway of her rooming house and huddled there, out of the rain, while the town of Dingle prepared for the opening ceremonies of the festival. It was quietly comic, with everyone evidently determined not to let the rain spoil things, and with the rain equally determined to come down as hard and fast as it possibly could.

A little band, formed of young boys and old men, their overcoats wrapped about them and their cloth caps pulled down over their foreheads, made several spirited passes up and down Strand Street. The band was not musically balanced, running to bugles and tin whistles and drums, but the old men and the youngsters made up in enthusiasm what they lacked in musical ability. They marched to and fro, playing with spirit and coming close to the desired tunes, and then the rain would pour down more furiously than before and would scatter their ranks, with the band's members scurrying or hobbling, depending upon their age, to take cover in doorways and pubs.

"And isn't it a horrid thing, to have rain on a night like this?" a woman demanded. "Eight o'clock it is, and in thirty minutes' time the Rose herself will sail across the harbor, and we should all of us be there to welcome her. But who'll be turning out on a night like this? And it's sad it'll be for Dingle if there's a bad showing at the pier."

The populace had no intention of making a bad showing. Rain or no rain, Ellen saw, the local people were determined to give the Rose of Tralee a fine and proper welcome.
By eight-thirty men and women and children were filtering
down to the foot of Strand Street to stand exposed to the elements in the little harbor. In spite of herself she was drawn
along in their wake. She bundled up warmly—the rain was
chilling, and there was a strong wind behind it—and followed the crowd. Her feet were cold and wet, and drops of
rain lashed at her face and trickled down over her wet skin.
It seemed a great deal to endure for the dubious thrill of a
fireworks display and a glimpse of the Rose of Tralee. She had
seen the girl—a beautiful girl, admittedly; a Belfast colleen
whose father had gone north from Kenmare some years before she was born—had seen her crowned in Tralee to the
joyous shouts of the assembled multitude. A beautiful girl,
to be sure, but surely one glimpse of the Rose of Tralee was
enough, wasn't it?

> *She was lovely and fair as the roses of summer*
> *Yet 'twas not her beauty alone that won me*
> *Ah now 'twas the truth in her eyes gently dawning*
> *That made me love Mary, the Rose of Tralee*

They had played the song incessantly at Tralee, with every
band piping it interminably through the streets of the town.
And now the Dingle band, tuneless but inspired, was giving
the familiar melody yet another run-through. She winced at
the missed notes and tortured rhythm.

To her left, a freckled little girl was talking earnestly with
her mother. "Now we'd better be getting home," the woman

said. "The rain coming down so hard, and you just over a cold."

"But mother," the child said, "I want to see the Rose."

"It's only a pretty lady, Bridie."

"Oh, no," the girl insisted. "It's a rose, a beautiful rose—"

A buzz went through the crowd. Someone had sighted the royal barge on the horizon. The welcoming committee was in place upon the wooden dock, and the first of the skyrockets was ignited and launched heavenward. It burst in a splash of fiery red, and a great cheer went up from the viewers.

"It's bad weather, but we'll give her a good welcome!"

"And why not? This is a day the lass will remember all her life, and the town of Dingle, too."

"If there'd only be an end to the bloody rain . . ."

Another skyrocket was touched off, and again the crowd burst into applause. Now, for the first time, Ellen could see the barge that bore the Rose of Tralee. She wondered how the girl must feel, sailing so slowly across Dingle Bay and into the harbor. The runners-up would be present, too—Miss Boston and Miss New York and Miss Dublin and Miss Liverpool, Irish beauties from throughout the world.

"Sure, and if it isn't Ellen Cameron, turned out in the rain to welcome the Rose!"

She spun at the thick brogue, at the mention of her name. And stood, open-mouthed, to stare into a familiar face.

It was David Clare.

Chapter 8

"It's you!"

"I'll not deny it."

"You're here—"

"In the flesh."

"I . . ."

She stood openmouthed while he shook his head solemnly. "I've had unusual welcomes before," he said, "but this seems sure to be the strangest. It's me, and I'm here, as you've observed. It's both of us, actually, and we're both here. Thee and me. We're both cold and wet, too, as far as that goes. At least I am, and you certainly *look* cold and wet. And lovely, incidentally. Hello, Ellen."

"But . . ." She caught her breath and swallowed. "What are you doing here?"

"Getting colder and wetter. By the minute. And waiting to see the Rose of Tralee dazzle us all with her beauty. See that one? A double-barreled skyrocket. I love fireworks, don't you?"

"I—"

"A friend of mine lost the tip of his third finger to a cannon cracker once. We didn't have a very safe-and-sane Fourth of July that year. But I still love fireworks. I'm incorrigible."

He studied her. "You somehow seem less than delighted to see me."

"That's not true!"

"Oh?"

"You just startled me," she said. She managed a smile. It was one thing to keep running across faces that looked familiar. It was another thing entirely to meet someone when you were not expecting to. "You took me by surprise," she said at length. "I never dreamed you would turn up in Dingle."

"Neither did I."

"When did you get here?"

"Less than an hour ago. I got off the bus and found a room—no mean feat, by the way—and decided to find you. And I thought to myself, now where would Ellen Cameron be on a rainy night? Out in the rain, I decided instantly. It seems I was right."

"Why did you come to Dingle?"

"I could say that the thought of the folk festival exerted a powerful magnetism that would not be denied. Or that it occurred to me that a visit to this particular part of the Gaeltacht might be in order before I head for Connemara." He lowered his eyes. "I could say either of those things, but neither one had much to do with my coming. I decided that I wanted to see you again, Ellen. I don't know whether I would have climbed the highest mountain or swum the deepest river—I'm not the world's greatest swimmer, as a matter of fact—but I was at least up to a bumpy bus ride from Dublin to Dingle." He looked down into her eyes. "You're cold and wet and more beautiful than ever," he said. "I'm glad I came, Ellen."

His hand found hers. They stood together in the rain,

hand in hand, as the Rose of Tralee's barge drew ever closer to the pier. The fireworks committee gave vent to an absolute orgy of skyrockets, anxious lest the Rose arrive before the last incendiary device had been properly exploded. Members of the crowd commented in delight upon the various rockets, groaning aloud when an occasional one proved to be a dud, shrieking with joy when an especially effective specimen burst into a riot of color overhead.

"They'll have to end with the American flag," David mused. "They always did back home."

"Silly. Do you think they make fireworks that explode into an Irish flag?"

"Probably not a great demand for that sort of thing. Say, look at that one! Sparks just missed the barge. Be a shame if the Rose got her eyebrows singed, wouldn't it?"

"You're a madman."

"No doubt of it. See those old fellows over there? They're jumping up and down every time a good one goes off. I'll bet they tossed a few real bombs in their youth. Shall we go, or do you really want to see the Rose?"

"I saw her in Tralee, but I'm not moving. This is too much fun."

"Rain and all?"

"Rain and all."

The barge docked, and the Rose accepted a bouquet of flowers—roses, of course—from one of the town dignitaries. Flashbulbs popped, and cheers came up from the crowd in waves. The band blared forth with "The Rose of Tralee." Ellen felt suddenly giddy, almost as she had felt the night at O'Donoghue's. But that time she had drunk oceans of stout, and tonight she had had nothing at all to drink. She was drunk on the cold salt air, on the rain, on the joy of the evening, on the presence, unexpected and deliciously welcome, of David.

The Rose entered one of the waiting cars, and each of the runners-up took a seat in another vehicle. Slowly the procession of cars moved out from the harbor and headed up Strand Street. A wave of people followed in its wake.

"You've seen the Rose," David said.

"I know. Wasn't she pretty?"

"Lovely. It's a pity you didn't have an ancestor from County Kerry. You'd walk away with it."

She flushed. "Oh, stop it!"

"You would. Ellen Cameron, the Rose of Tralee."

"Sure, and get off with your blarney!"

"Ah, and it's a good Irish tongue they've tucked in your pretty head! Did you learn to talk that way on your trip? Come on, let's find someplace where we can sit down and get out of the rain. There's a pub just up the street that looks decent."

"You've been here less than an hour and already you've picked out a pub?"

"We Clares don't waste time. First things first—that's what it says on the family crest. But in Latin, needless to say."

"Needless to say."

They shared a table in the snug, the little back room of the pub. The barman brought them pints of stout, and they sipped the dark brew slowly and talked without pause. She told him everything about her trip through the Irish countryside. This, she thought, was what she had been missing. All along she had been storing up impressions and reactions and had had no one to share them with. Now she let everything pour out, and he listened to every word, fascinated.

"It sounds as though you had a grand time, Ellen."

"I did. Oh, I did!"

"And got a lot out of it."

"I used up all my tapes and bought more and used them up too. I'm fresh out now. And I've learned, oh, I don't know how many songs. I won't be able to use all of them, but—"

"I don't just mean music. I mean—oh, the perspective a person gets on a trip like yours. The sense of the country. Even a sense of self."

She nodded. "Yes. I know what you mean."

"That could turn out to be even more valuable than the songs."

"I think it will."

He took her hand in his, and their eyes met. She held his glance for a moment, then lowered her eyes. She thought of the way she had told herself over and over again that she would never seen him again, that she had been no more to him than a pleasant companion for a few days and evenings in Dublin, a break from a dull September. But now she knew that she had meant more to him than that. He had come all the way from Dublin just to see her. She thought back to that morning, remembering how she had very nearly gone directly to Shannon, bypassing Dingle completely. Her landlady's words had changed her mind for her, and if she hadn't listened to the woman, if she hadn't come to Dingle according to plan, she might never have seen David again.

She shivered at the thought. What a horrid joke that would have been! She might have spent the rest of her life remembering him, wondering what ever had happened to him, never knowing that he had cared for her as much as she cared for him. *The road not taken,* she thought.

"Penny," he said.

She looked at him, puzzled.

"For your thoughts. Or are they worth a great deal more than that? If so, name a price. You certainly seemed lost there for a minute."

"Oh," she said. "I was just thinking."

"Of what?"

"Nothing important. What's that music?"

"They're having a songfest in the town square. Not the competition—that's tomorrow afternoon and evening. Just a few hardy souls gathering in the rain and singing their heads off."

"It sounds nearby."

"Want to have a look?"

"I'd like to."

"Drink up. We might as well get wet again."

The singing, as it turned out, was not near them at all. The city fathers had set up loudspeakers throughout the town, and the music was being carried over them. They walked blindly at first, trying to trace the source of the sound, until David stopped a man and obtained directions to the songfest. The rain had let up somewhat, and they walked arm in arm through the narrow streets to the public square. A small stage had been improvised there, and a giant of a man stood in its center, microphone in hand, singing a Republican anthem at top volume.

"This is where you hear the rousing ones," David told her. "All year long a man will tend his crops and sit in front of his fire and thank the Lord that the war's over. But give him a festive occasion and a few extra drinks from a jar of punch, and he'll be ready to lead an army into the Six Counties, and singing his head off about it. Then the next morning it's back to work again."

The song ended, and the huge, bushy-haired man introduced a pair of singers from County Monaghan who launched into a driving rock 'n' roll number made popular by the Beatles. It seemed so out of character to Ellen that she began laughing aloud.

"Just perfect for a folk festival," she said.

"But that's the whole point! Don't you see? Folk music isn't all neatly labeled and put in a drawer over here. The people aren't even apt to think of it as a separate category. It's just music, and anyone'll sing any songs he happens to like, and at any time. Oh, there are folk-music purists here, I suppose, like anywhere else. And you won't hear any rock 'n' roll at the competition tomorrow. But when it's just a case of a batch of people standing in the rain and singing, anything's liable to come out."

She stood beside him, clutching his arm with one hand and her purse with the other. From time to time they chatted easily, then lapsed into equally comfortable long silences while they listened to the music and watched the crowd around them.

"I wish I knew more about you," he said at one point.

"You know all there is to know."

"Do I? I don't know who's waiting for you back in the States."

"No one."

"Are you sure?"

"Only my agent, and his interest is limited to a percentage of my income. Is that the sort of interest you had in mind?"

"No."

"Then there's no one."

"Honestly?"

"Honestly. Do you really want to know more about me?" She shrugged. "There's very little to know, I'm afraid. Wait, I have an idea . . ."

"What are you getting at?"

"My passport," she said, fishing it out from her purse. "This will tell you everything there is to know about me. Age, height, weight, place of birth, color of eyes, color of hair—"

"I already know that."

"Well, all those vital statistics." She handed it to him. "Read on and discover the real Ellen Cameron."

"'Name, Ellen Cameron,'" he read aloud. "No middle name?"

"They never gave me one. Isn't that sad?"

"You were deprived. 'Place of birth, Belvedere, New Hampshire.' Well, I am learning things, after all. I thought you were a New York girl."

"Ever since college. There's not much happening in Belvedere."

"Are your parents there?"

"Buried there. My father died when I was small—I can hardly remember him—and mother died while I was at school."

"I'm sorry."

"Read on, sir."

"'Date of birth'—ah, you're, let's see now, twenty-four? A satisfactory age. 'Height, five feet five inches.' Just tall enough for the top of your head to fit under my chin. That's a more romantic way of looking at it, don't you think?"

"Infinitely so."

"'Weight, a hundred and seventeen pounds, five shillings and sixpence—'"

"It doesn't say that!"

"Well, skip the change, then. Just a good armful, that's all." He flourished the passport. "You know," he said, "I have an idea. A very good idea."

"Where are you going?"

He moved swiftly through the crowd and vaulted easily up onto the stage. He spoke in an undertone to the bushy-haired giant, who nodded and smiled and handed him the microphone.

"We're in for a rare treat tonight," he announced. "A professional folk singer has come all the way from New York City to sing for us. Her name" —he consulted the passport— "is Ellen Cameron. Her place of birth is Belvedere, New Hampshire, and her height and weight are a secret. And now she's going to honor us with a few songs."

There was a roar of applause. She shook her head at him, and he beckoned to her, and she sighed, shrugged, and gave in, joining him on the stage. The applause filled the night air.

"I'll never forgive you for this," she told him in an undertone. "I can't sing tonight."

"Of course you can. You're among friends."

"I'm going to have to learn not to trust you."

"Never trust anyone."

"I don't even have a guitar . . ."

But the man with the bushy hair was presenting her with one, and she took it and curved her fingers over the strings.

David slipped her passport into his pocket and dropped lightly down from the stage. "I'll be listening," he told her.

"I don't even know what to sing . . ."

"Anything you want."

"Well . . ."

"Go ahead!"

She set the microphone in its stand, let her fingers toy with the strings of the guitar, and then, at last, began to sing . . .

"I think I hate you," she said.

"That's sad. Because I think . . ."

"Yes?"

They were walking together down Strand Street toward her hotel. He had lit a cigarette. He passed it to her, and she drew on it, then returned it to him. The singing was still going on, and the loudspeakers made it sound as though the music were bouncing all around them. It was raining lightly again, but she did not mind the rain. She had sung half a dozen songs on the little stage, with the audience eager for more, and she did not really hate him at all, she loved him, and he had almost told her that he loved her, and she thought her heart was going to burst from it all.

"I wonder if it'll rain tomorrow."

"Probably," she said.

"If it doesn't, maybe we can go to the beach."

"Is the water warm enough for swimming?"

"I don't think so, but we can stretch out on the sand and watch the waves. Maybe we could pack a lunch and eat it on the beach."

"I haven't done that in ages."

"Sound like fun?"

"Uh-huh."

"Oh . . ."

"Something the matter?"

"Well, you'll be needing this sooner or later." He handed her passport to her. "I almost forgot to give it back to you."

"I wouldn't have been able to leave Ireland."

"No, you'd have to stay."

I wouldn't mind, she thought. *I wouldn't mind at all.*

At the door of her hotel they stopped and turned to face one another. "I'll pick you up after breakfast," he said. "If the weather's good, maybe we can go down to the beach. We should be able to buy sandwiches at one of the cafés. I'll bring a blanket to sit on. Or if it's raining again we can find something else to do."

"All right."

"Ellen . . ."

"There are people around."

"Do you care?"

"I should, shouldn't I?" She looked at him, then let her eyelids drop shut. "No," she said. "No, I don't care."

He kissed her. She snuggled up close to him and let her arms slide around his neck. He was so tall, she thought, and so strong, and his mouth was on hers and his arms around her and . . .

"I'd better go."

"If you don't go now I won't want to let you go at all."

"And I won't want to. Oh, David . . ."

He kissed her gently, then released her. "Tomorrow morning, after breakfast. Good night, Ellen."

"Good night."

He loves me, she thought, floating deliriously up the stairs. *I love him and he loves me.* She wanted to burst into song, wanted to shout her news from the rooftops.

I won't be able to sleep, she thought, slipping out of her clothes and into her bed. *I won't be able to sleep, because I am in love and the thought will keep me awake all night and . . .*

She closed her eyes and slept like a lamb.

Chapter 9

When she awoke the sunlight was streaming in through her window. She blinked at it and rubbed sleep from her eyes. The sky was cloudless, the day ideal for the beach. She dressed quickly and went downstairs for breakfast, sharing a table with Sara Trevelyan.

The Cornish schoolteacher was filled with plans of her own. There was a shop in town where bicycles could be rented, she told Ellen, and she intended to hire a cycle for the day and cycle north and west, exploring the remnants of prehistoric Ireland, the old earthen forts that stood as relics of ages long past.

"And I do want to see this," she said, passing her guidebook to Ellen. "Gallarus Oratory. One of the most perfect and best preserved early-Christian church buildings in Ireland, unless this booklet is telling me lies. See how perfectly shaped it is? Like a boat turned topside-down. And there's not a drop of mortar holding those stones in place, or so says the book. 'Carefully fitted together and completely watertight after more than a thousand years.' Can you imagine that?"

"It sounds remarkable."

"I'd like to see it." The older woman smiled. "I don't suppose you'd care to keep an old lady company, would you?"

"Oh . . ."

"It might be a pleasant trip for two. And it doesn't look as though it's about to rain, although I certainly don't trust this country in that respect. Do you like to cycle?"

"I haven't in years. I'd love to go, but—"

"You have other plans."

She nodded. "A young man I met in Dublin. He turned up in Dingle last night. It was quite unexpected. He asked me to go to the beach with him today."

"How grand! I'm sure that will be more enjoyable than a trip through the countryside with an old lady who talks too much. An Irish boy?"

"American."

"Ah. And he chased all across the country after you, did he? I'm sure you'll enjoy yourselves. I'd ask you to bring back a few pretty shells for me, but I suspect you'll have better things on your mind. Oh, you're blushing! Quite becoming, I assure you. I didn't know young ladies blushed in this modern age. I'm happy to see that they still do. I hope your young gentleman is worthy of you, Ellen."

A few tables away, the Koenigs were methodically working their way through a breakfast of eggs and sausages. The doctor's wife was a plump woman with dyed blond hair and a vacant, faintly bovine expression. The two children, both boys, showed no great resemblance to either parent. They were ten or twelve years old, Ellen guessed, and she wondered if children that age were capable of appreciating the greater delights of foreign travel. At the moment they seemed totally preoccupied with their food.

She wondered again where she might have seen Koenig. He did look familiar, there was no getting around it. Probably, as he had suggested, she had passed him in the street once in New York or Philadelphia. And yet she couldn't avoid the feeling that she had seen him more recently than that, in Tralee or Dublin . . .

She finished her breakfast, then went outside to smoke a cigarette and wait for David. He appeared just a few minutes after ten, a large paper sack in one hand, a blanket folded over his arm.

"A glorious day," he announced. "The beach beckons."

"It does indeed."

"I hope you like ham sandwiches."

"I'm mad for ham sandwiches."

"And I had them fill a Thermos bottle with coffee. You wouldn't believe how hard it is to find a Thermos bottle in Dingle. They seem to call them something else here, and storekeepers gave me the blankest of stares. So I had to explain just what it was that I wanted. Something to keep coffee hot, I said. One man presented me with a portable gas stove. Communication became impossible. I persisted. At last I triumphed. See what I go through for your sake, sweet Ellen?"

"You're a wonderful madman."

"I'm David the Rambler from Clare. I'm Kelly the Boy from Kilann. I'm taking a beautiful young lady to the beach. Ready?"

"Ready when you are, C.B."

"Onward!"

She sat on the blanket, her knees tucked beneath her. David was at the water's edge, his arm curved to send a flat stone skipping over the surface of the sea. He turned and walked to join her.

"Overcast already," he said. "I think it's going to rain."

"It does look that way."

"At least we had a few hours of sunshine. Is there any of that coffee left?"

She poured him a cup. "It's beautiful here."

"Yes."

"I love the shore. There's something positively hypnotic about the waves rolling in. Like a campfire. I can sit and stare at a campfire for hours and never say a word. David?"

"What?"

"I was thinking."

"Will a penny buy your thoughts this time?"

"You can have them free of charge. I was thinking that I don't really have to go to Berlin." He looked at her, puzzled, and she averted her eyes and rushed on. "It's not really a very important festival," she said. "It's an honor to be chosen, and I don't suppose the State Department would be elated if I failed to show up, but they'd barely miss me. I don't have a very important part in the proceedings. They could get along without me."

"But I thought you were so excited about it . . ."

"I was." She fumbled for a cigarette, and he scratched a match, cupping his hands to shield the flame from the wind. She drew on the cigarette, hoping she could find the right words, hoping she would not sound forward to him. "I was very excited about Berlin," she said. "But since then I've had enough folk music to last me awhile. I don't think I'm up to the rush and bustle of another festival. It would be a whole new country to get used to, and tons of people, and no sleep and all that singing, and I don't really feel equal to it."

"What would you do? Go back to New York?"

"No."

"Then . . ."

She took a deep breath. "I thought I might . . . oh, I thought maybe I could come to Connemara with you." She paused, and the silence was overpowering. "There's just no way to say this without sounding dreadful, is there? I don't want to leave Ireland. I'm enjoying myself too much. And I'd love to see Connemara. The things you've told me about the area make it sound magnificent. Maybe I could even learn Irish myself. I know I'd be able to pick up an enormous amount of Gaelic music. I could buy more tape and come back with some really exciting material. Stuff no one's even touched so far. And . . ."

She went on, parading all the reasons she could think of before him, talking as much to convince herself as to convince him. *I just don't want to leave him,* she thought. *I'm afraid, afraid I won't see him again. And I can't give him up . . .*

When she finished he got slowly to his feet. She watched him move slowly to the water's edge. He bent over and scooped up a handful of small stones. One by one he skipped them out to sea. After a few moments she rose and walked forward to stand by his side.

"I think you should go to Berlin," he said slowly.

She didn't say anything.

"Ellen, there's nothing I'd like more than to have you with me in Connemara. I hadn't even thought of it until you mentioned it. I hadn't dared. I only knew how I felt about you, you see. I couldn't be sure that you felt the same way about me."

"Oh, David . . ."

His hands found her shoulders, and his eyes sought hers. "But you have to go to Berlin. You say you don't want to now, and I'm sure you don't, but if you pass up this chance you'll be sorry later. You'd start to regret it the minute we got to Connemara. You'd wonder what sort of an opportunity you were passing up. You'd keep thinking about it, and you'd start to see me as a man who was already getting in the way of your career—"

"Oh, don't be silly!"

"It's the truth. You do have to go to Berlin, you know. And Berlin won't last forever. How long is it, a week? You could come back to Ireland as soon as the festival is over. Unless you've decided by then that you don't want to see me."

"That won't happen." She swallowed. "Would you want me to come?"

"More than anything."

He kissed her. She felt warm and secure in his arms, and yet there was a feeling of awkwardness between them that had not been present the night before. She had been too forward, she told herself. She had made a suggestion that it was not her place to make, and he had tactfully but definitely rejected it, and she felt personally rejected in the bargain. Now they were awkward with each other, and it might take them time to get over it.

She felt a drop of rain on her hand, then another on her forehead. "I think it's starting to rain," she said.

"Yes, I just felt a drop."

"I suppose we'd better get back to town."

"Yes, I suppose so."

He shook the sand out of the blanket, folded it neatly, and slung it over his arm. She took his hand, and they headed slowly back toward town.

*   *   *

They each needed to be alone, and both of them recognized this. She went to her room after making plans to meet him in an hour or so. She sat for a few minutes at her window, watching the rain pour down on the streets of Dingle. After a while she opened her guitar case and sat on the edge of her bed, playing the instrument softly, not singing now but merely playing old melodies on the guitar and letting her thoughts drift with the rhythms of the music.

She was still playing when Sara Trevelyan entered the room. "Don't stop on my account," the teacher said. "You play beautifully. I thought I might listen for a moment or two."

"How was your expedition?"

"Ill-fated, I'm afraid. I did reach Gallarus Oratory, and it looked every bit as remarkable as the photograph. Extraordinary structure! But I only had a few minutes there, when a look at the sky told me that this country was about to be favored with a bit more rain. Fortunately I started back right away. I did get rained upon, but I missed the worst of it. And I also proved to myself that I'm too old to be pedaling a bike up and down hills. How was your day at the beach?"

"All right."

"No more than all right? Well. Let me leave you alone, Ellen. I think I'll lie down in my room for an hour or two. These old bones could do with a rest. And do play that guitar. I enjoy listening to you."

But Ellen did not return to the guitar after the older woman left the room. Instead she put it back in its case and sat on her bed, staring moodily about. She picked up her purse, dumped it out on the bed, and sifted through its contents idly. She looked at her passport, remembering how she had presented it to David the night before. "Everything there is to know about me. Age, height, weight, place of birth, color of hair, color of eyes . . ."

Was that all she was, the sum total of those few facts?

She opened the passport and read the dry data to herself. Such an important document, she thought. And she peered at her own face in the passport photograph. ("A full-face shot, no larger than three inches by three inches, no smaller than two and one-half inches by two and one-half inches; both ears must show.") It certainly did not flatter her, she thought. But then she had never taken a very good picture. They'd had several sittings to get a portrait shot of her for use on her second record album, and she had never been particularly satisfied with the picture eventually chosen.

She started to close the passport, then noticed that the corner of the photograph had come loose. That was wrong, she thought. They sealed the photo to the passport, and it had to remain that way. She poked the corner back into place and it sprang persistently loose again. She wetted her finger with the tip of her tongue, touched her fingertip to the back of the loose corner, and sighed in dismay when the entire photograph came loose altogether.

Now what was she supposed to do? Probably the simplest thing would be to get some glue and put the silly thing back where it belonged. But would that be considered tampering with her passport? Maybe she was supposed to present herself at the nearest American consulate—wherever *that* might be—and have them laminate the photo in place according to their own particular methods. But what a load of red tape that would involve!

She looked at the passport and then at the troublesome photo, and then gaped in astonishment at a third article, which she had not seen before. It had been lodged in back of the photo, and now it was on her bedspread, very small, but suddenly alarmingly prominent.

She recognized it at once.

It was microfilm, a small square of microfilm, and it had been carefully hidden behind her passport photograph.

Chapter 10

Slowly, as if in a dream, she got to her feet and crossed her room. She closed her door and turned the key in the lock. She felt dizzy and thought that she might faint. She sagged against the door, clutching at it for support, until she felt strong enough to walk back across the room and sink onto her bed.

Her mind worked furiously. Everything was suddenly falling into place, every piece interlocking neatly in her mind. She could see the whole picture very clearly now, and it left her with a sick feeling at the pit of her stomach and a patch of dryness at the back of her throat. She looked at her hands; her fingers were shaking far more violently than they had done that last night in London, after the mugging.

The mugging. Of course—that had been part of it, the start of it. It had seemed odd, even then, that two men would stalk her carefully all the way through Soho and halfway to her door simply to make a grab for her purse. The few pounds it was likely to contain was hardly adequate compensation for their trouble. But they had not wanted money. They were trying even then to get hold of her passport. The passport had been in her other purse. Otherwise they would have fitted the microfilm into it that very night, and then the next morning they would have found some clever way to return it to her. Perhaps a man might pose as a detective and explain that it had been found in a gutter somewhere. They would have found a way, and in a few weeks the microfilm would reach its destination in Berlin.

But why had they chosen her? She studied the piece of film, wishing she had some way of knowing what it contained. Why her? Well, there were several reasons she could think of. She was headed for Berlin and was scheduled to arrive there on a definite flight at a definite time. And she was traveling at the behest of the United States Department of State, and at the invitation of the West German government. Those circumstances combined to make her an ideal unwitting courier for whatever secret information the microfilm contained. She would get a cursory customs inspection at the worst, and her passport would barely receive a second glance.

And then, in Berlin, the receiver would find a way to get his hands on her passport. The microfilm would be removed, the photo returned to its place, and she would go back to New York without having had the slightest notion that she had played a role in a game of espionage.

With trembling hands she managed to get a cigarette from her pack. It took her three matches to get the thing lit, and then she puffed nervously on it, stabbing it out in an ashtray after a few unsatisfying drags.

The face she had seen in Cork! She had thought it was nothing more than a case of nerves when the thin man with the long face appeared there. But it had not been her imagination. The man was just who he appeared to be, the same man who had choked her in London. And he was following her, biding his time, making certain that he could keep tabs on her. He hadn't tried to steal her passport this time.

Because it had not been necessary.

Another man had already set her up for the kill—

She reached for her cigarettes again, then pushed the pack furiously aside. How could she have been such a fool, such an utter and complete fool? She remembered the first meeting with David at the pub in Dublin, the smooth way he had managed to pick her up, the immediate interest he had taken in her. Of course he had been interested. It wasn't her looks or her voice or her personality or anything else about her that had interested him. It was the pure desire to make her a part of his little game of espionage. The whirlwind courtship in Dublin made it infinitely easier for him to keep her under surveillance. No need to have men following her, not when David himself could stay with her for hours at a time.

And then he had appeared in Dingle. She winced at the words she had spoken to him, at the great willingness she had shown to be played for a fool. She had actually believed that he had crossed the country for love of her. Love? Hardly that. It was in Dingle, her last stop in Ireland, where he would plant the microfilm in her passport. Then she would be out of the country in a flash and in Berlin in another flash, and that would be the last she would ever see of him.

"I think you should go to Berlin," he had said. "You have to go to Berlin. If you pass up this chance you'll be sorry later. You'd keep thinking about it, and you'd start to see me as a man who was already getting in the way of your career . . ."

She felt tears forming at the backs of her eyes, and she steeled herself and blinked them back. Of course he had insisted she go to Berlin—he wasn't interested in smuggling spy secrets into County Galway. No wonder her words had shocked him. And she thought of what would have happened if she hadn't spotted the film. She would have gone on to Berlin, just as he wanted, and then, fool that she was, she would have come right back to Ireland. And she would have gone to Connemara, anxious to see him, head over heels in love with him, but he would not have been there. He'd be out of the country, probably, and laughing his head off at the silly girl folk singer who'd been stupid enough to fall for every line he handed her.

She shook her head, almost unable to believe it. She had always felt herself to be a good judge of people, had prided herself in her ability to size people up quickly. This time she had fallen flat on her face. It seemed impossible that he could have taken her in so completely. She had honestly felt that she knew him well, and now it seemed that she had not known him at all.

"Everything there is to know about me. Age, height, weight..." Her precious little speech was coming back to haunt her now. That must have floored him, she thought; she had actually been so considerate as to hand him her passport without his even asking.

Or had that been a hint, when he gave her that line about knowing so little about her? If she hadn't brought out the passport, maybe that would have been his next line. "Let's have a look at your passport, Miss. I'd like to check your vital statistics, if you don't mind." Except, of course, that he would have phrased it more glibly than that. How delighted he must have been when she saved him the trouble! And then he had simply leaped up onto the stage to introduce her, and while she stood up there singing her head off, he held on to her passport for her—and slipped the microfilm into it.

But what could she do now?

She knew the answer to that readily enough. All she had to do was do nothing at all, hide the microfilm somewhere, glue the photo to her passport once again, and somehow get through the weekend. Then, once she got to Shannon, she could find someone and turn the microfilm over to him. An Irish customs official, perhaps, or an American consul. Was there a consulate at Shannon? She didn't know, but at least she could find someone there who would help her.

But of course, David would accompany her to the plane! She hadn't realized it before, but obviously he wouldn't let her out of his sight until she was on the plane bound for Berlin. And if she found some excuse to get rid of him, it was a sure bet that he would have someone else follow her. Like the man from London, the man she had glimpsed in Cork, the long-faced knife-thin man with piercing eyes.

She shivered. How could she get through the weekend? It wouldn't be possible for her to act natural with David. How could she let him kiss her now? How could she even walk at his side without breaking out in a cold sweat?

No. He would know at a glance, would know that she knew before she had spoken half a dozen sentences to him. And if he knew that she knew, if he realized that she would not smuggle the microfilm for him, that she would instead go to the authorities . . .

Why, he would kill her.

She looked again at her hands, held them out in front of her. She was surprised to note that her fingers did not tremble at all now. She was oddly calm, inexplicably calm in the face of the thought. She ran it through her mind as one of a series of interesting, even notable facts: it was raining outside, ontogeny recapitulates phylogeny, the square of the hypotenuse is equal to the sum of the squares of the other two sides, and he would kill her.

She tried to imagine it and could not; the image she had formed of him was so utterly incompatible with that of a killer that it would have been laughable if she had been capable of laughter. He *would* kill her, though, and probably without a second thought, without feeling anything at all. Because he was not what he had seemed to be. He had sat singing Irish songs with her, had stood skipping stones at the sea, but he was not really the kind of man who did these things. He was some sort of spy. He was a man involved with the men who had mugged her in London, he was a secret agent, a spy, he was . . .

She did not know what he was. She knew only books and movies, Richard Burton in a shabby trench coat, Sean Connery pressing dashboard buttons and sending pursuers spinning off the road. Eric Ambler, the Orient Express, knives and guns and strangling, newspaper headlines, a crazy montage of unreality.

She had to run. She had to get away, but David would be coming for her soon, and she had to get away, but how and why and where and oh, God, what was she going to do?

She had to talk to someone. She started for the door, got halfway to it, then halted abruptly and covered her face with her hands. She didn't even know whom to talk to. There was only one person in Ireland that she had come to know and trust, and that person was David, and he was the one person above all whom she could not trust, ever. She had to talk to someone, but whom?

Dr. Koenig? He at least was a fellow American, and he was a professional man, probably well traveled. He ought to know something, ought to be able to give her some sort of advice. She reached for the door, then drew back from it as though the doorknob were hot. She remembered how he had looked familiar to her, how she was certain she had seen him recently, perhaps in Tralee. And how, in spite of his denial, the feeling had persisted.

Maybe she had been right. Maybe he *was* someone she had seen before. Maybe he had kept an eye on her in Tralee. Maybe the "wife and children" were a blind. Maybe he was one of David's men.

Who else was there? The priest, she thought, the priest from Africa who had been so nice to her on the plane. But he was off visiting family in County Clare, and that was no closer than Shannon Airport itself. But he might have helped her if he had been around. He had impressed her as the sort of man who knew how to handle difficult situations. He had helped her with her luggage, and he could have helped her now, but there was no way on earth for her to get in touch with him.

Sara Trevelyan? Even the old Cornish woman could be one of David's gang, she thought, and then she pushed the thought from her mind. Miss Trevelyan, at least, was the woman she seemed to be. No one would recruit as a spy an old lady with aching bones who rode a bicycle up mountain roads.

Of course, she might be made up to look older than she really was. And Ellen hadn't actually seen her on the bicycle. And . . .

Oh, it was nonsense!

She unlocked her door, hurried down the hall to Sara Trevelyan's room. The door was shut. She knocked.

"Yes?"

"It's Ellen Cameron. I have to talk with you."

"I was just resting . . ."

She opened the door, knowing it was improper to do so, knowing too that propriety was no longer relevant. She closed the door and locked it, then turned to the old woman who was sitting on her bed with both pillows propped up behind her.

"Oh, dear," Sara Trevelyan said. "Something's gone amiss, hasn't it? Poor child. Don't tell me you're having a bit of trouble with your young gentleman?"

"More than a bit. It's—" She looked down at her hands, still clutching the passport and microfilm and photograph. "I'm in danger," she said aloud, testing the unfamiliar word on her tongue. And, again, "I'm in danger . . . ."

The older woman heard the story all the way through, paying very careful attention, nodding and clucking her tongue, putting occasional questions. "Oh, dear," she said, when Ellen had finished. "Yes, I do believe you *are* in danger, aren't you? I don't know what to tell you, Ellen. I'd say that you should go straight to the police, but I don't know just what sort of police force they have here. I shouldn't think a town this size would have a very elaborate police department, should you?"

"No."

"I've lived all my life in a town not very much larger than this one, and I can't help thinking of our own police. Just a handful of rural constables, actually. Very good at starting stalled motor cars and such, but not quite in James Bond's league. Not at all. I think . . ."

"Yes?"

"I should think you ought to get out of Dingle at once,

Ellen. I wouldn't even stop to pack my luggage. I'd abandon everything and take the first bus to Tralee, and change there for Shannon. You're certain to find someone at the airport who'll be likely to know what to do. And you'll be safe there." Sara Trevelyan frowned. "That's the most important thing, truly. Not the secret documents or whatever that little patch of plastic might be. But saving your own neck."

"I can't believe—" She broke off.

"Can't believe what?"

"That he'd really hurt me. Or kill me."

"Perhaps you had better believe it."

"Yes."

For a moment neither of them said anything. And then she heard a voice calling up the staircase, a familiar voice, a warm, strong, tender voice. "Ellen? Are you there?"

David's voice.

She said, "Oh, Lord, he's here. What am I going to do?"

"You certainly can't see him."

"No, I can't. I can't—"

"Stay right where you are," Sara Trevelyan said, getting to her feet. "I'll tell him you've left and give him a message to meet you. Be calm, Ellen. Everything's going to be all right, you know."

She stood at the door, waiting, listening, while the older woman walked to the staircase and down the stairs to the first floor.

"I beg your pardon, but did I hear you calling Miss Cameron?"

"Yes. Is she in?"

"No, she's not. You must be David Clare? She gave me a

message for you. She went around the corner to the café for a cup of tea. She said you would know which café she meant."

"Should I wait here for her?"

"No, she wanted you to meet her there, if you would."

"I will. And thanks very much."

The older woman appeared at the doorway, a smile of amusement upon her lips. "I surprise myself," she said. "Who would have thought I'd reveal such a talent for deception, and so late in life at that? Give him a minute or two to get round the corner, Ellen. And get your purse from your room. Don't try to carry anything else. I'll bring your other belongings over to this room and keep them for you until I hear from you. You know how to find the bus station?"

"Yes."

"Go straight to it. There probably won't be a bus leaving for an hour or more, but you can buy your ticket and hide there. You might try concealing yourself in the W.C. until your bus is ready. Not many men are up to storming into a ladies' lavatory."

"I don't know how to thank you."

"Oh, goodness, I haven't really done anything, now have I? Get your purse, you don't want to waste a minute now. I wish I hadn't turned in my bicycle. You could ride it to the bus station. Hurry, now."

She went to her room, snatched up her purse, dumped the passport and photo and microfilm into it. She rushed down the stairs, then hesitated for a moment in the doorway, afraid to step outside for fear that he would still be waiting there. She took a deep breath, held it for a moment, then walked quickly outside.

It was still raining, only a light but persistent drizzle now. She looked carefully both ways and saw no one who looked at all familiar. She turned to her left, toward the bus station, and began to walk as quickly as she could. She wanted to run, but if she ran people would notice her and wonder why she was running. And there were probably other men of David's in town; she didn't dare attract their attention.

The bus station. Just a few blocks farther, and she would get a ticket to Tralee and find out when the bus was leaving. She would do as Sara Trevelyan had suggested, would hide in the ladies' restroom until the bus was due to leave. Should she buy a ticket clear through to Shannon? It might save her time at the Tralee station . . .

No, she decided against it. Once they realized she was gone they would be sure to make inquiries at the bus station, and she didn't want David to know her ultimate destination. He might guess it anyway, of course, but there was no sense in making it easier for him. Once she was out of Dingle, the most dangerous part would be over. Of course, he could take a fast car and get to Shannon before her. He could be waiting there when she arrived, but she would stay in crowds, stay close to other people, and maybe he would be unable to do anything.

"Ellen!"

Her heart froze.

"Ellen, where are you going? You weren't at the café. Wait a minute."

She turned her head quickly. He was on the other side of the street, just half a block back. He stepped to the curb now, waiting for the traffic to clear so that he could come after her.

She ran.

"Ellen! Hey, hold on—where are you going? Ellen!"

She ran like a thief.

Chapter 11

Out of breath, exhausted, she sagged against the side of a building and listened to the leaden pounding of her heart. She did not know how long she had been running or precisely where she had run to. Hers had been a mad dash for freedom, turning corners at random, dashing across streets just inches ahead of passing cars and cycles, racing blindly on with the conviction that nothing ahead of her could be half so horrible as the menace behind her.

And now she had lost him. She was free now, free and clear. He had been unable to follow her, and she was free.

But not safe.

She found a cigarette in her purse, a Woodbine, and she scratched a match and lit it. Not safe at all, she thought. Because the bus station still provided the only way out of town, and she didn't dare go to it. He knew now, knew for certain that the game was over once and for all. He would not have to bother with deception any longer. Instead he would be desperate. He would have to get the scrap of microfilm from her, and he would have to make sure that she never told anyone what she had learned about him.

And what did that mean? A gun? A knife? A pair of strong, huge hands around her throat, squeezing, squeezing?

She closed her eyes, shuddered, then opened them again

and took another urgent drag on the cigarette. Whatever part of town she was in, it was probable that she was within half a dozen blocks of the bus station. Dingle was a small town, small enough so that she could be sure of reaching the bus terminal within a few minutes, walking. But now she didn't dare go there. He would be having the place watched, either by himself or someone else. The moment she turned up there, someone would come after her. And she would never be able to run away again. She could barely stay on her feet, let alone walk anywhere. Running was out of the question for the time being.

She wondered, now that it was forever too late, if she could have bluffed David. She could have avoided seeing him as much as possible, could have pleaded a headache and spent as much time as possible in her room. And the alleged headache might have helped cover her change in mood. If she acted differently with him, she could have blamed it on the way she felt. Perhaps she could have carried it off, perhaps she could have kept him from ever suspecting that she knew the truth.

Could she have done it? Perhaps—she didn't know. But now it was pointless to think about it, because now he could not help being aware of her knowledge. She had run away. It had saved her for the time being, but at the same time it had let David know exactly where she stood, exactly how much she knew.

Where could she go? The bus station was not safe. Neither was her room. The cafés and pubs of Dingle seemed equally unsafe. If she stayed where she was, sooner or later David or one of his agents would see her. Surely someone had a car, and they could cruise up and down the few streets of Dingle until they saw her. And then . . .

A church, she thought. She could wander into one of the churches and hide there. She wondered if you could still claim sanctuary, as criminals had in medieval times. Perhaps not, but would they dare to come after her in a church?

She began walking. Strand Street and the downtown section of Dingle were to her left, she was fairly sure, so she turned to the right and started slowly up the street. Perhaps there would be a church nearby. But she couldn't stay huddled in a church forever. Sooner or later she would have to come out. Sooner or later she would have to take a chance and find some way to get out of Dingle.

A gust of wind blew up, driving sheets of rain into her. Already the sky was growing dark. In an hour or so it would be nightfall, and the protective cloak of darkness would be at once a hazard and a blessing. It would be harder for them to find her in the dark, but it would also be more difficult for her to find her way around. And where was she going to spend the night? She would grow hungry and thirsty and tired, and there was no place she could go for food or drink or rest.

A car approached, and she instinctively turned her face away from the street to avoid being recognized. The car slowed. David, she thought, and her heart sank. She couldn't run any more. She just couldn't run any more.

The car stopped. She turned in spite of herself and saw a priest climb out of the front seat of a small red Triumph sedan. Relief flooded over her in a wave. It was not David, it was a priest, and he could even help her find the church. And he would be someone to talk to, someone who would know what to do, how to help her.

"Miss? I'm afraid I've lost my way. Could you direct me to Saint Michael's Church?"

She wanted to laugh—it was he who wanted directions. And then she looked at him again, a tall man with a broad forehead and strong features, and her jaw dropped in recognition.

The same spark of recognition illuminated his eyes. "Why, don't I know you? Let me see—why, on the plane from London, wasn't that it? Now you'd be the folk singer who nearly lost her guitar. You're Ellen Cameron, aren't you?"

"Father Farrell!"

"Yes, I thought I recognized you." He smiled. "The girl who laughed so politely at my little stories. Why, this is a coincidence, isn't it? Or did you say you were coming to Dingle? I seem to remember that you did, now that I think of it. And how have you enjoyed your trip to Ireland? I've had a grand time myself. All my family at home, and now I've come visiting relatives here in Dingle whom I haven't seen in years." He saw her face, then, and his eyes changed expression. "Why, you're all upset, child. Is something the matter?"

"Oh, Father," she said. She was panting for breath now, unable to speak. "Oh . . ."

"Why, you poor child, you're in a state of sheer terror! Now nothing can possibly be that bad. I know you're not a Catholic, but perhaps you'd care to talk about it anyway. It so often helps to discuss one's problems with another, and we priests have had worlds of practice listening."

"I don't know where to begin."

"Start anywhere you wish. But let's not stand out in the rain while we talk. My brother made me the loan of his car.

Rather a flashy thing for a man of the cloth, wouldn't you say? But come, get in and we'll talk about it. Come, Ellen."

He led her around to the right-hand side, held the door for her, then walked around the little car and got behind the wheel. He turned the key in the ignition and began driving. For several moments she did not trust herself to speak.

"You can tell me," he said.

And then the words poured out of her.

Chapter 12

The little red sedan made its way slowly along one of the narrow winding roads to the north of Dingle town. Ellen sat slumped in her seat, exhausted. Father Farrell, evidently quite practiced at hearing confessions, had listened to her full story with a sympathetic ear. She had thought at first that it might be almost too preposterous to tell him. He was, after all, a gentle priest from rural Ireland, a man who had spent the past few years living as a missionary in a tiny African community. What would he know of the world of spies and international intrigue? And how could he help her?

But he soon showed that he was able to understand this sort of thing. "It sounds to me as though you are in very serious trouble," he told her. "You still have your passport? And the photograph, and the scrap of film?"

"Yes."

"Well, that's fortunate. Because I suspect that film is very valuable, or they would never have gone to so much trouble. You were wise not to go to the police."

"Perhaps I should go to them now, Father."

"No, I think not." He hesitated. "The police in our smaller cities are an unsophisticated lot, Ellen. They're country folk, and they're used to dealing with the sort of crimes that occur in villages. Spies and stolen plans are a wee bit over their heads."

"But they could contact someone—"

"Would they?" He shook his head. "It's a sad thing for a fellow Irishman to say, but I wouldn't trust them if I were you. Small-town gardai are traditionally suspicious of foreigners, you see. They would very likely detain you. At best they would order your immediate deportation, probably shipping you back to New York."

"At least I'd be safe there."

"Perhaps. But you wouldn't get much in the way of protection before you were deported, and things could go badly for you. This Clare fellow seems daring and resourceful and quite ruthless. And suppose that you were deported? What do you think your own countrymen would do?"

"I don't understand."

He slowed the car to permit a small boy to lead a band of sheep across the road. Then, resuming speed, he said, "Consider how it will look to the American officials. They will find out that you met David Clare at a pub in Dublin, that you consorted willingly with him for several days, that the two of you met again in Dingle. From their point of view, it will look as though you were a willing agent of the spy gang all the way."

"But that's insane!"

"Of course it is, child, but will they see it that way? I doubt it. Remember, you were invited to Berlin. Then and only then you decided to come to Ireland, and you met with Clare the very first day in Dublin. It will look like collusion to them, don't you see? And then they'll suspect that the two of you had a falling out or that you developed cold feet at the last moment. And that that's why you turned in the film."

"What would they do?"

He shrugged. "Different governments operate differently. I suspect at the least they would suspend your passport indefinitely and forbid you to travel. And of course they would put you through a long and grueling interrogation. And meanwhile you would have exposed yourself to a great deal of danger. Do you see what I mean?"

"Yes, but . . ."

"But what?"

"But I still don't know what I can do to avoid it. I can't see David again. He knows now, you see. And I can't go on to Berlin. I certainly can't give them the film. I wouldn't do anything like that!"

"Of course you wouldn't."

"Then what can I do?"

He considered this for a moment, guiding the little car through a narrow passage, then heading up a sharp incline toward the peak of a little hill. She reached for a cigarette, then paused to ask him if he minded her smoking. He said that he did not. She lit the cigarette and rolled down the window part way so that the little car would not become thick with smoke.

"Ellen?"

"Yes?"

"I've been thinking about your situation. I'm not as worldly as I might be, to be sure, but I have traveled a bit. And even a missionary got a taste of the unrest in Africa, the interplay of political forces. So I may be able to advise you and to help you."

She said nothing.

"The first step is to make you safe from harm. That's the most important consideration for the time being. You need a place to hide for the night. A place where you can sleep safely while I go back to Dingle and try to learn something more about your situation. I can move around town without arousing suspicions, you see. Clare and his gang would never suspect a black-robed Irish priest of having an interest in their dirty little scheme."

"It would be dangerous for you."

"I think not. And with any luck at all I should be able to come up with some sort of solution. Now if there were only a place where you could hide, a sanctuary from the elements . . ."

Sanctuary. She said, "Gallarus Oratory!"

"What's that?"

"Gallarus Oratory," she repeated. "Oh, Miss Trevelyan was there just this morning." Quickly she described the ancient structure. "Of course, it's a major tourist attraction, but I don't think there would be people there at night, do you?"

"I doubt it. Probably few enough there this afternoon, in weather like this."

"Well, it should be comfortable. It's watertight after a thousand years, it says so in the guide book. And David would never think of looking for me there."

"You never mentioned it to him?"

"I can't remember. I might have said that Miss Trevelyan was going there, but nothing beyond that. He wouldn't have any idea that I would think to go there. And he wouldn't suspect that I would go anywhere in a car. I don't have a car, and I don't know anyone with a car, so he wouldn't realize that I would be able to get out of Dingle."

"It does sound good," he said. "Do you know how to find it?"

"No. It's somewhere north of Dingle, but I don't—"

"There's a county map in the glove box, I believe. Can you reach it for me?"

She passed him the map. He slowed the car to a stop at the side of the road and unfolded the map, holding it against the steering wheel and studying it intently. "Gallarus Oratory," he said. "Gallarus Oratory. Well, here's Dingle, and the roads north—ah, here it is now, Gallarus Oratory. Yes, I should think we can find it with little difficulty."

"It shouldn't be far. Miss Trevelyan reached it by bicycle."

"No, not far at all. We've even come in the right direction, though we'll want to take the next road off to the left." He refolded the map, and she returned it to the glove compartment. He started the engine and eased the car back onto the road.

She was quick to recognize the oratory. It was just like the picture in Sara Trevelyan's guide book, and it *did* look like an inverted rowboat. The state of preservation was remarkable.

The little building was quite deserted. He parked the car, and they walked to the entranceway through the rain. The doorway was just high enough for her to get through without stooping, and Father Farrell had to bend down to get inside. It was dark within, and damp, although air and light filtered through from a deeply splayed loophole window at the rear of the structure. The building was small on the inside, about fifteen feet by ten. The floor was composed of bare earth, packed down hard over the years. She would be quite safe here, she thought. No one would think to look for her here.

"I've a blanket in the car," he said. "I'll fetch it for you. And my mother packed me a lunch that I never did get around to eating. I think you should be comfortable here."

She waited. He returned with a heavy blanket and a large brown paper bag. Seeing him, she thought of David that morning, with his own blanket over his arm and their picnic lunch in one hand. She had been so happy then, so very much in love. And only a matter of hours ago.

She felt as though she had lived years since then.

"I think you'll be comfortable."

"I'm sure I will."

"It may get a bit cold."

"I'll be all right."

He spread the blanket on the ground for her. "A remarkable building," he said. "How old is it, do you happen to know?"

"I'm not sure. Over a thousand years."

"Extraordinary that a pagan culture could produce such a structure. And just by piling one stone on top of another." He shook his head in wonder. "I'm sure you'll be safe here. Does anyone know of your discovery besides David?"

"I assume the other members of his gang. I don't know how many of them there are."

"Besides them, I mean. Did you tell the woman everything?"

"Sara Trevelyan? Yes, I did."

"And anyone else?"

"No. Does it matter?"

"It might," he said. "I should think that the fewer people who know, the better off you are. I think there may be a way out for you that wouldn't involve all that trouble with the authorities." He smiled sadly. "As a priest, perhaps I should advise you to cooperate with the authorities. But the Irish clergy have a long history of opposition to government. We were hunted down like common criminals in the old days, you know. During the Penal Law days, they paid five pounds for the head of a priest, and no questions asked. And after Cromwell came the situation didn't improve all that much either, from what I've heard. So I'm not too great a believer in trusting governmental authority without question. You may be better off avoiding them entirely. You might even have to go on to Berlin as planned."

"But how could I do that? I can't let them get the film."

"There should be a way out. I'll have to think about it, Ellen. I'm going back to Dingle now. I'll spend the night there, wander about, see what I can learn. I'll come by for you in the morning. Do you think you'll be all right here until then?"

"I'm sure I will."

"You won't be nervous, all alone here in the middle of nowhere?"

"No, I'll be all right." She swallowed. "I was a lot more nervous in Dingle. I'll be fine now."

After he had left, after she could no longer hear the putt-putt of the little red Triumph sedan, she walked to the narrow doorway and looked out at the countryside. Night was coming fast. She wondered, now, how she would be able to stand it. She was exhausted but felt she would be unable to sleep. She had not eaten in hours, and yet the thought of food left her with a weak feeling in the pit of her stomach.

She ran her hands over the thick stone walls of the oratory.

One of the most perfect and well-preserved of early-Christian church buildings in Ireland—that was how Sara Trevelyan's guide book had described it. Now, though, she saw it not as an architectural masterpiece but as a temporary refuge. She might have been moved by the building, coming on it as a tourist, but in her present situation she could not react to it in that fashion. She was grateful for it as a place to hide in, a roof over her head, a secure corner where she could hide and wait for Father Farrell.

It was growing dark. Would animals enter the place at night? At least, she thought, she was safe from snakes. There really weren't any in Ireland, venomous or otherwise. Not, she had learned, because of the work of good St. Patrick; there had never been snakes in Ireland, as the island had separated from the European land mass before snakes had evolved, and so they had never appeared there.

An interesting fact, she thought, but one that would not do much to help her get through the night. What other animals might come around? She didn't know; the only sort she had seen in the country were domestic animals, cows and horses and pigs and goats and sheep, wandering at will in the country roads and over the green countryside. She didn't suppose she had anything to fear from them.

A fire would keep animals away, but how could she build one? There was nothing inside the oratory, no wood, and any wood lying about outside would be far too wet to burn. Besides, she realized, a fire might do more harm than good. It could attract attention, and that was the last thing she wanted.

She walked through near darkness to the blanket Father Farrell had spread out upon the floor for her. She opened the paper bag and examined three thick ham sandwiches. She took a bite of one and chewed it and had trouble swallowing it. She put the sandwiches away and closed the bag.

She stretched out. The ground was very hard. She looked around at darkness. She was tired, so tired . . .

It was still pitch dark when she awoke, surprised that she had fallen asleep. She was hungry now and ate all three sandwiches. She wished there were something to drink. She went outside. It had stopped raining, but the sky was still fully overcast, with neither the moon nor the stars visible. She wondered what time it was.

Her thoughts kept her company for the next few hours. They were bad companions at best. She thought about David Clare, and how she had felt about him, and what he really was. She was furious with him, angrier still at herself for being so easily taken in.

She cried bitterly, fought against the tears, then gave in and cried some more. She felt more foolish than ever, sitting outside an ancient building in the dark of an Irish night, far from everyone, far from home, crying like a child. But she went on crying, and when the tears stopped she felt somehow better, more sure of herself.

After a while she lay down on the blanket again and slept. She tossed with dreams, all of them bad, and when she awoke a second time it was morning and the sun's rays swept in through the little doorway. She was hungry again and wished that she had thought to save one of the sandwiches for the morning.

She went outside, into the chilly dawn, holding the blanket around her shoulders. She stood there waiting for Father Farrell, and when she heard the first sounds of an automobile engine she started down the hill toward the road to greet him. Then she realized that it might not be him, that it could in fact be anybody, and she withdrew into the embracing sanctuary of the oratory until the red Triumph came into view.

He brought breakfast—some soft rolls, some cold sausage, a whole quart of milk. After she had eaten they left the oratory and got into his car.

"Some bad news first," he said. "I'm afraid it confirms all the worst that you've thought about Clare. That woman you'd spoken with ..."

"Sara Trevelyan?"

He nodded. "There was an auto accident in town. A woman was struck down by a car—"

"Oh, no!"

"I'm afraid it's true. The woman was Miss Trevelyan, and it seems she was killed instantly. Hit-and-run, of course; the police have no clue to the driver." He shook his head sadly. "They assume it was an accident. You and I know better. It seems evident that the poor woman was purposely and deliberately murdered and that your David Clare had a hand in it."

"That's—that's horrid! Why would he ..."

"You spoke to her. He must have known it. His kind don't like to leave witnesses alive, I understand. And so he killed her. He's probably killed before, and one murder more or less ..."

She hardly listened to the priest's words. It was almost impossible to believe that the gentle retired schoolteacher from Cornwall was dead. She had been so intensely alive, so young and vital in spite of her years, that it seemed incredible that she could be dead.

And the thought of David's doing the deed, of David at the wheel of a speeding car, bearing down on the woman, the car's bumper hurtling into her, lifting her up, hurling her forward . . .

She could not bear to think of it.

David. She saw now that she had all along been hoping against hope that somehow she could have made a mistake, that he was innocent. In spite of everything, a portion of her mind had still loved him in a way, had still hoped to find him vindicated. She had never been entirely able to believe that he was what he now appeared to be, a spy and a killer.

But it was true. Already an innocent person had been sacrificed to him. And he would kill her just as easily, just as dispassionately.

"I've come up with a plan," Father Farrell was saying. "I've had all night to work it out, and I think it may go fairly well. You see, it's necessary for you to get away from here as quickly as you possibly can. And it's also absolutely necessary for you to avoid contact with the authorities. But at the same time you don't want to be giving aid of any sort to Clare and his crew of villains. I think I've found an answer."

"What?"

"I'll drive you to Shannon. I'll stay with you there, keep you out of sight until it's time for your plane to leave. You'll get on your flight to Berlin right on schedule."

"But . . ."

"What could be simpler? While you're in the air, I'll return to Dingle. I'm sure I can contrive to have Clare arrested, at least detained for the time being. After all, I'm an Irish priest, and he's a foreigner. I can invent some excuse, I'm sure. Say that he tried to pick my pocket. Accuse him of public blasphemy." His eyes twinkled. "Almost any excuse will do, actually. It's a far cry from the days when Priests were hunted for sport. The authorities are Irish now, and they listen when we speak. I won't have to put Clare away for any great length of time. Just long enough so that you can get to Berlin before he gets in touch with his colleagues over there."

"And then?"

"Then they'll have no way to know that the plans are changed. They'll snatch your passport one way or another, according to plan. They'll open it up and take out the scrap of film and find a way to return the passport to you. You'll do your part in the Berlin folk festival, receive a full measure of applause, no doubt, and then find your way back to New York." His eyes narrowed. "I fear you'll take bad memories of Ireland with you. But I hope they'll fade in time and that you'll remember the good things about our nation and forget the bad."

She thought for a moment. "There's one thing."

"What's that?"

"Well, I can't really pass on the information, can I? I mean, I wouldn't want to be a part of their spying. Don't you see?"

"Of course I see. And you won't."

"But . . ."

From a pocket he drew forth a small scrap of film similar in appearance to the one she had found beneath her passport photograph. "Just ordinary film," he announced. "But at first glance it looks quite like that devilish item from your passport. Of course, once they examine it through a viewer they'll know a mistake's been made, but even then they won't expect you've had anything to do with it. And in the meantime I'll forward the real microfilm to the American authorities. Anonymously, of course." He chuckled. "When the men in Berlin realize they've been had, it won't be you who comes in for their fire. They'll suspect Clare has done them out of the goods, and they'll probably come gunning for him. So you'll be entirely in the clear, and no one will ever connect you with what has happened."

"I see."

"I think it's a good plan, Ellen. Of course, I've not had much experience in this sort of thing, but I do think it might work."

"Yes," she said. "It might."

"There's no other way. You have to go to Berlin or you'll arouse suspicion. And you have to stay away from Clare. And of course, if there's nothing in your passport when you get to Berlin . . ."

"Yes. I understand."

"I brought a tube of glue," he said. "Let me have the passport and photo and all." She gave them to him. "And the piece of film," he added. "I'll want to get that to the right people."

She gave him the film, and he opened up the passport and went to work on it. "You might get the blanket from the building. And pick up any papers left behind."

"I forgot all about that."

She hurried back to the oratory, folded the blanket carefully, picked up the debris from last night's dinner and this morning's breakfast, stuffed everything into a paper bag, and carried the bag and blanket to the car. He opened the trunk and put everything inside, then handed her passport to her. "All set," he said. "I have the other piece of film, I'll take care of it. And I suspect it's time the two of us got started for Shannon. We'll take the northern route across the peninsula to Tralee. If he's thought to set up a roadblock, he'll have blocked the southern road. That's the more usual route, the one your bus took coming to Dingle. From Tralee we'll drive straight to Shannon."

"You could leave me in Tralee. I could take a bus . . ."

He touched her hand. "No chance of that," he said. "You're in trouble, and I'm going to help you get out of it. I'm on vacation, remember. My time is my own." His lips narrowed. "I can't think of a better way to spend it."

Chapter 13

From Gallarus Oratory they drove almost all the way back to Dingle town before cutting off to the left. Then they were on a rough, narrow road heading northeast between two groups of mountains. He pointed out the Brandon Mountains to their left, the Central Dingle range to the right.

"This is one of the prettiest drives in all of County Kerry," he told her. "There's a rough beauty to this peninsula that can't be surpassed anywhere in Ireland. They filmed *Playboy of the Western World* here, you know. In Inch, on the southern shore of Dingle peninsula. And the Blasket Islands are just offshore at the western tip of the peninsula. They're uninhabited now. They ran into a couple of bad fishing seasons, and in nineteen fifty-three the government moved all the islanders over to the mainland. But some of the folk still talk of returning to the islands again. They're a hardy people who only know a hard life. Long hours of work and little pleasure, and always the danger of shipwreck."

He talked easily, and she relaxed in her seat beside him and thought that everything was going to be all right now. She was having a nice ride, watching lovely scenery, safe in the company of this gentle priest. And it would all be over soon. Shannon, then Berlin, then New York—and it would be over, like a bad dream, and she would be safe.

And someday, she thought, she would quite forget David Clare.

> *I never shall marry*
> *I'll be no man's wife*
> *I'm bound to stay single*
> *All the days of my life*

"Have you spent much time in this part of the country?"

"Some," he said. "Family, you know. On my mother's side. It was a grand place to come in the summer, for the swimming and fishing."

"I suppose County Clare is very beautiful too."

"Oh, indeed."

"I suppose it takes a foreigner to appreciate an area, though. Don't you think so? A native is apt to take anyplace for granted. I know I'm that way at home. America's a grand country, and there are so many exciting places in it, and yet because I live there I rather take them for granted. I suppose you'd be that way yourself, in Ireland."

"Perhaps. I was more the sightseer in Africa than I am in my own native land."

"I guess everyone's that way." She looked out the window. The car had reached the summit of a hill, and she looked at the valley spread out below. Bare rocks, the lush green of the grass, the ribbons of piled stone fences, the stones arranged without mortar like the stones of Gallarus Oratory, though in a much less precise fashion.

"I suppose that's why you never visited the oratory before," she said.

"Pardon?"

"Oh, I mean that it's odd you never went to Gallarus Oratory before. If you weren't from Ireland, you'd probably have made a great point of seeing it on your first visit to Dingle. But instead you came here often and never did get to the oratory until last night."

"That's an interesting thought."

"And I'm the same way. I've lived in New York ever since graduation, and do you think I've ever been to the Statue of Liberty? No tourist would think of missing it, but I've never gone, and I probably never will get around to it. I keep meaning to, but I know I'll always be in New York and the statue will always be there, and so it's easy to put it off. Though I almost went a couple of years ago. Maybe you read about the time that some lunatics were going to blow it up? And the Washington Monument, and I forget what else?"

"Yes, it was in the Dublin papers. And then just recently some of my own countrymen blew up the Nelson Pillar in O'Connell Street, of course."

"I know. Anyway, after that happened—or after it didn't happen, I mean—well, I was going to go to the Statue of Liberty, because for a while it looked as though it might *not* be there forever. But I didn't. Did you have a subscription to the Dublin papers while you were in Africa?"

"Pardon me?"

"Well, you said the bomb scare was in the Dublin papers, but then you must have been in Tanzania at the time, mustn't you? Did you have a subscription or did a relative just send you the papers now and then?"

"Oh," he said. "Yes, that's it. My cousin sent me parcels from time to time, things one couldn't get where we were, and he'd use the papers as packing material. So I'd get to read them now and then. It kept me in touch after a fashion."

"It must be strange to be away so long."

"Yes."

She lapsed into silence. When she got home, she thought, she would have to go to the Statue of Liberty. She really meant it this time. She would go just like all the tourists, and she would walk up the steps inside and everything. Could you still walk up the arm? She seemed to remember that those stairs had long been closed, but she wasn't certain.

"Look at the view, Ellen."

"Oh, it's beautiful!"

"It is, isn't it? Aren't you ashamed of yourself, coming to such a beautiful country without a camera?"

"Oh, but I'm no photographer. And I did have my tape recorder. Oh, I almost forgot. You'll take care of my things, won't you? The guitar and the suitcase and the tape recorder? I won't need them in Berlin, I can borrow a guitar, but you'll ship them to me in New York?"

"I'll take care of everything."

"Oh, that's wonderful." She looked out the window, then glanced at him again. "How did you know I didn't bring a camera?"

"You told me."

"I did?" She frowned, unable to remember. "When?"

"On the plane. You made light of it at the time. Don't you remember?"

"It's funny, but I don't. I must have been chattering like a magpie that morning."

"You were upset over what had happened the night before."

"I must have been."

"And that may explain why you've forgotten talking about the camera. Your mind was on the purse-snatching incident, and so you don't remember what you'd said to me."

"That must be it." She sat for a few more moments in silence. Then she said, "I wonder what he's doing right now."

"Clare? Looking all over Dingle for you, I suspect."

"Probably."

"I didn't see him last night. I looked for him but didn't see him. I did see that Doctor Koenig, though. I wonder if he's in with Clare. It would be a good cover for him, traveling with wife and children . . ."

Her mouth opened, then snapped shut quickly. She looked away. She knew with absolute certainty that she had never mentioned Dr. Robert Koenig to Father Farrell. She might have been mistaken about the camera, that was possible, but she had never once mentioned the Philadelphia psychiatrist to him.

Then . . .

A phrase leaped at her: "Extraordinary that a pagan culture could produce such a structure." He had said that at Gallarus Oratory, when she told him the little stone building was about a thousand years old. But a pagan culture had *not* produced it—Ireland had been Christian for centuries when Gallarus Oratory was constructed. And an oratory was by definition a chapel, a place for meditation and prayer, and specifically Christian. A priest would certainly know that.

He was not a priest.

She struggled to remain calm. What else had he said? There was something else, something that had struck a wrong note at the time but that she had not paid much attention to.

About the persecution of priests in Ireland, how they were hunted during the days of the Penal Laws, how their lot did not improve too much under Cromwell. But that was all backwards! The persecution of Catholics began in earnest under Cromwell, and the Penal Laws did not come into being until long afterward, until William of Orange had defeated James II at the Battle of the Boyne, until the Irish under Patrick Sarsfield had finally capitulated at Limerick in 1691. He had the whole thing completely backwards, and it was not the mistake any Irishman would make, and certainly not an Irish priest.

He was not a priest!

He was talking, something about the scenery. She couldn't listen to his words. It came to her in a rush now. The very day after they had snatched her purse, Father Farrell had made contact with her. He had carefully managed to get the seat next to her on the plane. He had drawn her out, learned the full details of her itinerary in Ireland. And when there was the mistake about her luggage, he had managed to get his hands on her passport. All he had needed, really, was the luggage check—but he had specifically asked for her passport, and sent her off to the lunch counter while he removed the photo and inserted the scrap of microfilm and sealed the passport up again . . .

So it had been in her passport throughout her entire trip. That was why the long-faced man in Cork had made no attempt to snatch it. The work had already been done. They had only needed to keep her under surveillance, to make certain that she kept to her schedule and got to Berlin on time.

That was why Father Farrell had stayed out of sight in Dingle until after she discovered what was happening. Koenig could have told him—he must have overheard her talk with Sara Trevelyan and then passed the word to Farrell, who had come along to keep an eye on things. And then Farrell—she shouldn't think of him as *Father* Farrell now, he was no more a priest than she was—Farrell had come out of hiding and revealed himself, posing as her savior while he got his spy game back on the track again.

And she had blamed David!

Of course he wanted her to keep away from the police. Of course he wanted her to go to Berlin as scheduled while he stayed behind to "take care of everything." And the nonsense about substituting another piece of film for the original microfilm—that had been a neat bluff. She was certain that the original scrap of film was right back where it had been, underneath her passport photograph. And she would go to Berlin, just as he had planned in the first place, playing as blind a role in the game of espionage as ever.

And Sara Trevelyan—oh, God, she had sent him straight for the woman! "Did you talk with anyone else, child?" Of course he had to know; he had to find out just how many people he ought to kill. The poor woman! And David—had he done anything to David? Oh, God, she couldn't stand it! She wanted to scream. Her nerves were stretched so taut that she thought they would snap any minute.

No. She had to be calm, had to stay relaxed. That was her only chance. If she could keep him from knowing that she had seen through him, then perhaps she could get out of it all right. He would take her to Shannon, and once there she would find some way to get away from him, some way to reach the Irish or American authorities on her own—once she managed that, she would be in the clear. They could arrest

Farrell—and she wondered what his name really was—and she could turn over the microfilm and find David and . . .

David.

Oh, God, and she had suspected him, she had got everything wrong. Had Farrell killed him? If that had happened she could never forgive herself. She couldn't think about it, wouldn't let herself think about it. She had to be calm. She had to act the same way with Farrell, had to play along with him, had to keep him from guessing that she knew.

If only she were an actress instead of a singer. If only she were a better liar.

"Ellen? Something on your mind?"

"Oh, no. No, I was just looking at the scenery. It's really glorious, isn't it?"

"Yes, it is." He reached over to pat her hand paternally, and she could barely manage to keep from flinching away from him. "You're still nervous, aren't you?"

"I'm fine."

"Oh? You seemed nervous."

"It's just that I'm impatient to get to Shannon and out of the country. I keep worrying that he'll try to ambush us there." Lies, lies, and her voice sounded false to her own ears, and how could he fail to notice it? Oh, God!

"This is Conor Pass coming up. The view is glorious from here, Ellen. You can see Brandon Bay and Tralee Bay and Dingle Bay all from one spot. You can even see clear back to Dingle town when the visibility is right."

"It must be breathtaking."

"Oh, it is." He slowed the car. "Why don't we stop and have a look at it, Ellen?"

"We don't want to waste time . . ."

"Ah, but surely we can afford a minute?"

"David—"

"He doesn't even know you've left Dingle, child. And he'll never suspect we've taken this road. Sometimes days go by without anyone driving a car along this route. Everyone goes the short way. There's probably not another motor car within miles."

A shiver went through her like a sword.

The car slowed to a stop. "Come," he said, opening his door. "Let's have a look at the scenery."

She didn't want to get out of the car. She was afraid. But she couldn't argue with him, couldn't let him see that she was frightened. That would certainly tip him off, and she couldn't afford that.

She opened her door and got out of the car. She left her purse with the passport in it on the seat. He put the car in neutral, pulled up the hand brake, and left the car with the motor idling.

"This way," he said, taking her gently, gently by the hand. "A grand view, isn't it? That's Brandon Bay on the left and Tralee Bay on the right, and the stretch of sand between them is Rough Point. It looks like Italy turned upside-downs doesn't it?"

"Yes, it does."

"You're shaking, child. Not afraid of heights, are you?"

She wasn't, but she clutched at the straw. "I always have been. I can't help it—I get weak in the knees from looking down."

"Oh, it's a common fear," he said "One of the most common, I believe. I understand they call it acrophobia. Fear of great heights, and one of the most common of the irrational fears. Although it's not always irrational, is it?"

And, in the same conversational tone of voice, he said, "How long have you known, Ellen?"

"I don't understand . . ."

"You're not afraid of heights, you're afraid of me. And quite rightly so, I'm afraid. How did you guess? You're far too smart for your own good, child. You should have stayed stupid—you'd have saved your life that way. You could have gone to Berlin in perfect safety and never gotten into any trouble at all. But now you know, don't you? I must have made a slip or two along the way. The camera? Well, it doesn't matter, does it?"

She backed away from him, her hands out in front of her, her eyes wide in terror.

With a terrible smile on his lips, he moved toward her.

Chapter 14

There had to be a way out. She wouldn't die, couldn't die. There had to be a chance. The car—if she could get to the car, she could get away from him. The car was her only chance. But meanwhile he was coming for her, slowly, patiently, and he was going to kill her, and she had to stop him. One way or another she had to stop him.

She said, "You don't have to kill me."

"Don't I? Of course I do."

"No. No, if you kill me, then I can't take the microfilm to Berlin for you. But if you let me live I'll take it. Just as you planned. I'll take it, I'll let your men there take it from me, I'll never breathe a word of it to anyone. I swear . . ."

He shook his head sadly.

"I mean it. I'll do it, I'll do it perfectly, you can trust me. You can stay with me in Shannon and put me on the plane yourself. I couldn't possibly double-cross you that way because it would be easy for you to check on me. And then you could have someone meet the plane the moment it lands, and I'd give him the film right away. It would work—"

"No, Ellen."

"But why not?"

"You could tell the pilot. Or you could slip away from me in Shannon. You're a bright and resourceful girl, too much so for your own well-being. If only you had stayed stupid a day or two longer, then everything might have been different."

"I wouldn't try to get away from you. I—"

"And afterward, after it was over in Berlin, you would go straight to the American Embassy. You'd tell them names and descriptions and all sorts of things which I really don't want them to know. The less those people know about me, Ellen, the better I like it."

"Are you a Communist?"

He threw back his head and laughed. "Oh, come now! Certainly not. I'm afraid I'm far too fond of the things money buys to dream of a world without the profit motive. As a matter of fact, Ellen, it's possible that your scrap of film will wind up in American hands after all. It just depends who's prepared to pay the highest price for it. The Americans, the Russians, the Chinese—they'll all have a chance to bid against each other in Berlin. I'll be happy to do business with any of them."

He wasn't even a spy for patriotic reasons, she thought. That motive she might have sympathized with, but he was involved in all this spying and killing just to make a profit. That made him somehow more frightening and bloodless than ever. She could expect no mercy from him, and she knew it now. Her only chance was the car. And her only way of getting to the car, of having an opening, was to keep him talking. As long as she kept the conversation going she would be alive, and as long as she was alive there was a chance, however slight, that he would make a slip and give her an opening.

"How did you know, Ellen? The camera? That was a foolish mistake on my part. I searched your room last night, went through your luggage. So of course I knew that you had no camera with you, but I forgot how I'd learned as much. Is that what tipped you?"

"No."

"What, then?"

"Koenig. I never said a word to you about him, and then you mentioned him out of the blue. That was when I knew."

"Ah. Another mistake."

"You made other mistakes, too."

"Oh, did I?" He seemed amused. "Tell me about them. I'll have to learn to avoid them in the future."

She told him about the Penal Laws, how he had mixed up his history. And how he had made the mistake about Gallarus Oratory.

He nodded, interested. "An old fault of mine," he said. "When I get into a role, I have a lamentable tendency to carry it too far. I like the sound of my own voice too much, you see. Just a frustrated actor at heart, perhaps, but I tend to overdo things. You didn't suspect then?"

"No." And bitterly, she added, "I trusted you."

"You should never trust anyone, Ellen. Not even an Irish priest."

She remembered something he had just said. "You went to my room last night."

"Yes. It was a simple matter to walk in. No one looks twice at a priest in this country. God, how I loathe them! Like crows in their black garb. Evil crows. I was raised by Jesuits. Not in this country. On the Continent. A bunch of evil crows. A flock of them. 'God, S.J.' Hah!"

"Why did you go to my room?"

"To look around. And I had another errand there, child."

"Sara Trevelyan . . ."

He smiled. She had never seen such a hideous smile in her life. "Sara Trevelyan," he echoed. "Yes, I'm afraid so. Not a car accident at all, as it happens. That made a good story, don't you think? But a bit inconvenient to arrange. It was much easier to go to her room." He smiled the same evil smile again. "She let me in without a second thought. Why? Because I was a priest. Who would shut the door on a priest? She had no idea who I was or why I had come to her, but she let me in."

He was lost in the memory. He held his hands out in front of her and studied them intently. "I twisted her neck," he said slowly. "Like a chicken."

"Oh, God!"

Still smiling, he went on, "She fought me. She struggled well for so old a person. But I have very strong hands, and I strangled her slowly, very slowly. And all the while I looked into her eyes, and they were wide-open in terror, and then, do you know, they glazed over. It's remarkable the way that happens. The light went right out of her eyes, and the life went right out of her, and that was all. All."

She could barely breathe. The look in his eyes, the smile, the infinite calm with which he could speak so viciously. She had never met an utterly evil man before, had never experienced such a personality at close range. Only in books or at the movies—Richard Widmark pushing an old lady's wheelchair down a flight of stairs, that sort of thing. She had never really believed such scenes, had never honestly thought that there were people on earth who could kill in such a chilling, coldblooded fashion.

But she was standing before one now.

She said, "And David?"

"No. No, I went looking for him. He was never alone long

enough. I walked home behind him, to his rooming house. I had a knife for him, a very sharp knife. But there were people in the streets."

"Thank God!"

"Oh, don't give thanks, Ellen. It's a short reprieve at best. He knows little enough, but he knows you, and that means he knows too much. Dr. Koenig will be keeping him company today, and later this afternoon or evening the knife will find its mark. But you won't even know about it by then, will you?"

"If you kill me, how will you get the microfilm to Berlin?"

"Koenig's woman will take it in."

"His wife?"

"Not exactly his wife. A partner, let us say."

"Why didn't you have her take it in the first place?"

"I'm afraid they know her too well in Berlin. But with your passport I don't suppose she'll have much trouble. She fits your description rather well, you know. Doesn't look at all like you, but a passport description isn't a very precise thing, is it? Height and weight and that sort of thing. And passport photos never look like anyone very much, do they? It would have been more convenient to use you, Ellen. That's why we thought of it in the first place. But" —he shook his head sadly— "you've made that quite impossible, I'm afraid."

He took a step toward her. Again she backed away. His hands, his awful hands—she pictured them around poor Sara Trevelyan's neck, squeezing, and the picture made her sick to her stomach.

"You can't kill me."

"Oh, but I *can*. I have to, you see."

"No . . ."

"I've no choice." He smiled that smile again. He was enjoying this. Well, let him enjoy it, she thought fiercely. As long as he talked, as long as he went on talking, she was still alive. When she stopped talking and he grew bored, she would be in danger. It was like a cat with a mouse, she thought. As long as the mouse fought and scampered and struggled, the cat went on playing with it and the mouse went on living. But as soon as the mouse ceased to struggle, the cat would grow bored with the whole affair and end the game by eating the mouse.

He was the cat and she was the mouse and he was playing with her, enjoying her fear, her desperate attempts to talk herself free. And as long as he kept enjoying the game . . .

But mice never escaped, she thought. That was the only trouble. The game always ended the same way, with the cat devouring the mouse. The mouse never won.

"How shall I kill you, Ellen?"

A new twist for the game. "Oh, no," she stammered. "You have to let me live, you have to. I'll do anything. I'll do anything you want. I'll go to Berlin or disappear or hide or whatever on earth you want me to do. I'll do anything at all."

"Anything?"

"Anything," she said. Her hands moved, indicating her slender young body. His eyes traveled the length of her body, then moved upward again to her face.

And he began to laugh.

"Why, Ellen! I honestly think you mean it."

"I do. Anything—"

"Shame on you, child. Seeking to tempt a holy father to indulge in the sins of the flesh. May the Lord forgive you, child."

"Stop it!"

He roared with laughter. He came closer to her again. She backed away, and he circled to his right, hemming her in. The cliff was to her rear now. She could not back up much further or she would fall over its edge. And he was very close to her.

"But I think your charms are wasted on me, dear." He smiled. "I'm afraid that women don't interest me that way. The only way you can give me pleasure, dear Ellen, is by dying an interesting death."

She shivered. He wasn't human.

"And how shall I kill you? Help me decide."

"Please . . ."

"I thought of the knife," he said thoughtfully. "It's a beautiful knife. It's in the car, under the seat. A very long, very thin blade. Do you like knives, Ellen? Do you find them beautiful? A knife can be a very beautiful object, you know."

"You're insane!"

"Do you really think so?" The idea seemed to amuse him. "Perhaps. It's been suggested before. I don't let it bother me. I thought of the knife, Ellen, but I rejected it. There's a great deal of variety with a knife. It can be fast or slow, painful or relatively painless. But I don't think I like the knife, the more I think about it. Not for you. For David Clare, perhaps. Should I make it fast or slow for him?"

She didn't want to answer, didn't have the strength to answer, couldn't stand to listen to the filth he was spewing, much less reply to it. But she knew what happened to the mouse the moment the game became dull for the cat. So she said, "You don't have to kill him. He doesn't know a thing, not a thing. You can let him live—"

"Oh, no. Because he knows you, and if you don't turn up

he's going to find out why. And once he contacts the authorities, your passport won't be much good to us, will it? No, he'll have to die. With the knife. Quickly, I think. Why prolong it? We're prolonging your death, Ellen, by standing here and talking about it. It's not much fun, is it?"

"You're horrid!"

"Horrid. That's an interesting word. Like the little girl with the curl in the middle of her forehead. 'When she was bad, she was horrid.' That's how it goes, isn't it?"

"Yes."

"Could you sing it for me?"

"There's no tune."

"A pity. I've never heard you sing, Ellen. What song would you like to sing for me?"

She broke and started to cry. This seemed to delight him. He took another step closer.

"We haven't finished talking about your death, Ellen," he said. "Strangling, perhaps? I think that may be best. To strangle an old woman one night and a pretty young girl the next. Yes. I'll do it very slowly and watch your eyes all the while. Yes. That's better than shoving you over the cliff, don't you think? I'll do that later, after you're quite dead, but I thought of throwing you off alive, and I don't think that would do at all, do you? No, because there's no guarantee. It would cripple you, but it might not kill you, and I simply can't afford to have you left alive. This whole operation has taken very careful planning, dear. It has to be done properly, and so I think I shall strangle you after all, like your Cornish friend, and I think I've wasted enough time already, wouldn't you say? I think it's time for you to die, Ellen, and I'll watch your eyes turn, just as I watched hers turn last night, and you'll struggle, yes, yes you will, you'll struggle, and you won't really believe it's going to happen. All the while you'll think there's a way out, you'll think a bolt of lightning will come out of the clouds and strike me dead and you'll live. You'll invent all sorts of ways you can be saved, and while you go on dreaming of them my hands will be tightening, tightening, and I'll be looking into your pretty eyes, Ellen, and my hands will tighten and it will hurt you, it will hurt very badly, Ellen, and then while you go on dreaming all of a sudden you will stop, everything will stop for you, the world will stop for you, Ellen, and your eyes will turn and you'll go completely slack and you will be dead, Ellen, dear, dear child, little girl, dead—"

Just as his hands, curled like claws, reached for her, she lashed out. She ducked down and came at him in a rush, hands flailing out, her head butting him in the pit of the stomach. She took him completely by surprise—he fell, and she sprawled on the ground beside him. She scrambled to her feet, and then his hand hooked around her ankle and brought her crashing down.

"Oh, Ellen," he said. "So you'll make a fight of it . . ."

He had one hand on her ankle, the other hand higher up on her legs. She scrabbled at the ground with both hands, brought up fists full of dirt and tiny pebbles. She turned and threw the dirt at his face, and he let out a roar and rubbed furiously at his eyes with both hands. She pulled herself free and ran for the car.

But he was up and after her. He caught her, and when his cold hands touched her she almost gave up, almost quit, but something made her fight on. She spun away from him and kicked out, and he laughed and kept coming, and she kicked again and caught him in the pit of the stomach and he doubled up in pain, a moan escaping his lips.

For a moment she was frozen, almost unable to believe she had hurt him, unable to move now that the chance was hers. Then, as he was getting to his knees, she recovered herself and sprinted for the car. She almost ran around to the left-hand side, but then she remembered that the car had right-hand steering, and she got the door open and flung herself behind the wheel.

The motor was still running. She put the car in gear and pressed down upon the accelerator, and nothing happened, the motor roared but the car stayed in place. There was a moment of panic, and then she remembered the handbrake and released it, and the car leaped forward.

David, she had to find David!

She spun the car around in a tight U-turn. She made the turn all right, but then the tiny motor coughed and died, and he was racing toward her now, and she wasn't sure she knew how to start the car. She put the clutch in and turned the key and the starter whined and the engine caught, and he was grabbing at the door, clutching at the handle just as she fed the car gas and the car rushed forward again, pulling away from him, and when she looked in the mirror she saw him sprawled out on the road behind her, sprawled on his hands and knees while she sped away, safe, free.

She was safe.

She was alive, alive.

And he would not be able to come after her now. He had told her how deserted the road was, how days passed without another car appearing. He would be a long while on the road, and no one in Dingle would know what had happened. She could hurry back to Dingle. She could find David, somehow, and get him away from there. They would drive to Tralee and from Tralee to Shannon, and they would find someone, anyone, who could help them.

But they would have to hurry.

She checked the rear-view mirror. She could still see him, walking in the roadway behind her, covering the ground quickly in long, firm strides. He was coming after her on foot. She wanted to drive faster but didn't dare. She was on the wrong side, it felt crazy driving on the wrong side of the car and the wrong side of the road. And the road was so narrow, and there were hills, and she was afraid, God she was afraid.

No, she told herself. No, there was nothing to be afraid of. There was plenty of time. She had got away from him, that was the important thing. She was alive and she was free of him and he would never get near her again. That was the important thing. And David was innocent, David was really in love with her, David was hers, hers, and she would find him and he would drive the car and then she wouldn't have to do it any more, and she would be safe, she would be David's, everything would work out—

She saw the car in the rear-view mirror, a long way back. It wasn't fair, she thought. It wasn't fair. Hardly any traffic at all, days going by without a car, and now there was a car coming at just this time. It wasn't fair. She watched in the mirror as Farrell stepped easily to the side of the road and held up his hand toward the onrushing car.

Maybe it wouldn't stop for him. Maybe . . .

The car slowed, stopped. Farrell opened the door, got into the car.

Of course, she thought. Of course. And she burst out into

hysterical laughter, humorless and involuntary laughter. Of course. For who in Ireland would think of refusing a ride to a priest?

The car behind her began to move again Grimly, desperately she pressed down harder on the accelerator and urged the little red Triumph on toward Dingle and David.

Chapter 15

When she hit the outskirts of Dingle town she slowed down. Beads of sweat dotted her forehead and trickled down her arms to the backs of her hands. She was past fear now; she had lived with it too long and was now running on momentum and adrenalin. Somewhere in front of her was David. Somewhere behind her was Father Farrell—no, not Father Farrell, not even Farrell, but that would do until she knew his real name. Somewhere behind her was Farrell. She had not caught a glimpse of the car in a long while, and her first thought had been that the false priest had been unable to persuade his driver to match her speed. Now, the more she thought about it, the more certain she was that the car behind her had stopped. Farrell would not want an innocent citizen for company if he caught up with her. So he would make the driver stop the car, and then those hands, those horrid hands, would reach out for the man's throat . . .

That would explain why the car had dropped back out of sight. And she knew he would do the deed without a second thought. He would probably yearn to do it, for that matter. She had seen the light in his eyes, had heard the wildness in his voice when he told her how he would kill her, told her all of it in heart-stopping detail. She had cheated him out of the thrill of a murder, and he would be hungry to kill, anxious to take any life, and the man who gave him a ride would have been sacrificed to that hunger.

So he'd have a car of his own now. And what sort of car? She hadn't recognized it. It was one of those British automobiles designed like a 1954 Ford, and all of them looked quite alike to her. But whatever sort it was, whatever make, it was probably faster than the Triumph. It was certainly larger and likely to be more powerful.

So she didn't have much of a head start.

She went to his rooming house first, hardly daring to get out of the car but knowing it was the first place to look for him. She rushed up the stairs, calling his name, and got no answer; finally someone else, English and irritated, told her he had gone out.

She went to the cafés, the pubs. And found him at last in a pub a block off Strand Street, sitting in an armchair and drinking a pint of stout. He gaped at the sight of her and got up from the chair.

"Hurry!" she shouted. "Come with me, there's no time!"

"What on earth *happened* to you, Ellen? And what—"

"I'll explain later, there's no time, you've got to come." She was frantic. "I'll explain, please, hurry, there's a car out front, hurry, there's no time—"

A man on the other side of the room was out of his chair now, walking their way.

Koenig.

"Hurry!" she shrieked. She grabbed his arm, pulled him toward the door and the waiting car. "You drive," she said. "You're used to it, driving on the left, listen, I'm all flustered, I can't think straight. Listen—"

"I'll say you're flustered."

"David, drive. Drive as fast as you can. Drive out of town, drive to Tralee. Oh, God, Koenig's got a car, he's heading for it. Go, David. For God's sake . . ."

She stopped then, stopped because there were no words left, stopped because she had run out of breath, stopped because he had at last given up trying to get an explanation and was, thank the Lord, driving the car. He swung onto Strand Street, headed east, out of town.

He said, later, "Tralee?"

"Yes, I guess so. That direction, anyway. And as fast as you can."

"This isn't exactly the fastest car on earth."

"I know."

"I'll do what I can. Ellen, are you all right? Is everything . . ."

"I'm all right."

"I looked for you. When you ran yesterday I didn't know what to think. Are you sure you're okay now?"

"Yes."

"And will you tell me what this is all about?"

"In a few minutes." She turned in her seat, looked out through the rear window. She could not see Koenig's car yet.

"I'll explain it all," she said. She took a deep breath, held it, let it out very slowly. "In just a few minutes, David. I have to catch my breath. And oh, I have some things to tell you, and they won't be easy to tell . . . ."

She sat back in her seat, a cigarette in her hand. She had finished, and he had not spoken a word throughout the recital. She was waiting for him to say something. The little red car was flying along the road to Tralee. David was a good driver, and he had the throttle wide-open and his hands poised lightly but firmly on the steering wheel. He drove intently, his eyes darting from the road to the rear-view mirror to the road again, his concentration absolute.

For a hysterical moment she thought that he had not believed a word she said—that he was convinced she was insane and was humoring her. She could prove it, she thought. She could get her passport from her purse and peel off the photograph and show him the microfilm. She could prove it if she had to, and—

But he said, "You poor kid. You poor, frightened kid."

"I'm all right now."

"What you must have gone through. It's a miracle you're alive, Ellen. A miracle."

"It'll be more of a miracle if we're both alive in another few hours."

"Are they behind us?"

"I can't see them, but with all the twists in this road they could be fifty yards behind us and I wouldn't know it." She turned to face forward once again. "Have you caught a glimpse of them in the mirror?"

"Not yet. But Koenig has an American car, I saw that much. We've got an advantage on the winding roads, but we're dead if we ever hit the straightaway for any length of time. That's where his car's power will come in handy. Do you have a map handy?"

"In the glove compartment. Farrell used it yesterday, to find the oratory. David?"

"What?"

"You're not . . . mad at me?"

He looked at her. "For what?"

"For what I thought. That you—you know."

"Why should I be mad at you? It was the sensible way for you to figure it from where you stood."

"No it wasn't. I should have known better."

"You added up two and two and got four. Anything else would have been a surprise. To tell you the truth, it's remarkable that you tumbled to Farrell at all. He had a perfect setup, Ellen. He never had to win your confidence. All he had to do was appear before you and act priestly, and he had it made. It might have been tougher for him if you were a Catholic. But how many priests have you known personally?"

"None."

"Exactly. All you had was a general image of what a priest was, and any time he deviated from that image you would only think that he was an offbeat sort of priest, a little more colorful than the stereotype. No, I can't blame you for trusting him before me. You're just lucky to have tumbled to him at all."

"Lucky?" She frowned. "I don't know if it was lucky or not. Suppose I had played along with him because I didn't know any better. I'd have gone on to Berlin and then home. I might have helped him by doing his dirty work for him, but I wouldn't even have known that." She glanced nervously at the rear window again. "At least I'd have got out alive."

"Uh-huh. Of course, Koenig would have stuck a knife in me, somewhere along the way . . ."

"Oh, I forgot!"

"And you wouldn't have got off alive in the long run, anyway. He couldn't leave you around. You'd know too much, and if anything ever went sour they could trace you and get

back to him through you. No, I'm afraid you would have had
an accident arranged for you in Berlin, Ellen." His voice hardened. "From what you've said, he's a man who likes killing.
History's filled with men like that. They only kill for a reason,
but somehow they can always find a reason. You're lucky you
found out what was happening, and lucky you got away from
him at Conor Pass. If you can be lucky one more time, we
might get out of this."

She didn't say anything. Shakily she got two cigarettes
from her purse. They were the last of her cigarettes. She lit
them both and gave one to David, then crumpled the pack
and tossed it out the window.

"Littering," he said.

"Fifty-dollar fine in New York."

"No fine here, but criminal. And criminally wasteful, unless you've got more cigarettes."

"No, I don't."

"Well, neither do I. We could have shared one and kept
another for later. I don't suppose it matters. Is that a car behind me?"

She spun in her seat and leaned over it to look out the
window. A big car, American, was hurtling toward them.

"It's him," she said.

"Koenig?"

"Yes."

"Alone?"

"No, there's somebody with him. I can't see the car now,
it's around the bend. Wait, there it is again. It's not Farrell.
I don't know where he is, but that's a woman with Koenig.
Probably his wife, or whatever she is. The one who was going
to use my passport."

"Can you still see them?"

"Yes. No, not now."

He swung the wheel hard to the right, spun off on a nar-row unpaved road. The road dipped down a hill, then curved off to the left.

"Where are we going?"

"I don't know," he said, "but the Tralee road's no good, not with them that close to us. The road's too straight and we can't get enough speed out of this buggy. They'd be on us in no time." He took a sudden curve without slackening speed, and the car careened wildly but held the road. "These little monsters are good on roads like this one," he said. "They're built to take it. I wonder if he saw us turn off."

"I don't know. I wasn't looking just then, I don't know."

"Be a sweet piece of luck if he didn't. If he stayed on the Tralee road and passed us by. Of course, this road probably does a loop-the-loop and deposits us right back on the Tralee road anyway. Have you got that map yet?"

She got it and opened it.

"Try to figure out where the hell we are and where we're going. I think we can forget about Shannon. Farrell's too smart to leave that open. He'll have got to a phone by now, and there will be men waiting in and around Shannon for us. If we can find a way, I'd just as soon bypass Tralee completely."

"And go where?"

"I don't know. Cork or Dublin—there are consulates both places. The embassy in Dublin, for that matter. Just so we stay away from them. That's the only thing that matters." He drew on his cigarette, blew out a cloud of thick bluish smoke. "Like the IRA flying columns in the Tan War. They didn't have to win battles. All they had to do was stay in the field. As long as they existed, they were a thorn in the side of the British. They had to hit and run, but most important they had to preserve themselves. That was their most important objective."

"And it's ours, too?"

He nodded. "Right. It doesn't matter how soon we get the film to the proper authorities. There's no rush. Farrell and his men can't get anywhere until they get us. You've got the film, and they're stuck without it. As long as we can keep away from them, as long as we can stay alive, we're ahead of the game."

"David . . ."

"What?"

"Koenig saw us turn onto this road."

"How do you know?"

"Because I just saw him behind us. He's a good way back. The last hill, there was a long view of the road behind us, and I saw him."

"You're sure it was his car?"

"Positive."

"Check the map. Where does this road go?"

She found the road. "I think this is it. It doesn't go anywhere in particular. It passes Tralee about seven or eight miles to the south—"

"Good."

"—and then goes to some place called Castlemaine. From there you can take a big road north to Tralee or south to Killorglin . . ."

"Forget that. Does the little road continue?"

"Uh-huh. It goes to Farranfore and Scartaglen, and then it sort of trickles off. I don't know how good this map is. But there are other little roads from Scartaglen."

"It's our route, then. Wherever it goes. It doesn't really

matter where we go, just so we stick to the back roads. Just so the gas holds out. We've got about half a tank, and I think we ought to get close to thirty miles to the gallon."

"That much?"

"I think that's what the ads say. No, wait a minute, we won't get anything like that." He stopped talking long enough to spin the car precariously around a hairpin curve. "If this weren't so harrowing, it almost would be fun. Remember the roller coaster when you were a kid? Where was I? Oh. We'll get about twenty to the gallon, driving like this. Wide-open throttle and plenty of hills, twenty will be good. Half a tank—I wonder how much a tank holds? Maybe ten gallons. So figure we have five gallons, which means we can go a hundred miles before it's time to look for a petrol station."

"And then what?"

"I don't know. I suppose we worry about that when we come to it. How are you fixed for money?"

"Not much cash. Some traveler's checks. You?"

"Not much cash and no traveler's checks. My money's in my room. This is a fine mess you've got us in, Stanley."

"I know."

"Can you see Koenig behind us?"

"No."

"I wonder if there are any special buttons on the dash-board. We could leave a smokescreen behind us or an oil film on the road. I'd love to send Koenig spinning off the side of a cliff, phony wife and all. Sean Connery always has a batch of buttons to push. All I can see are the windshield wipers and the headlights. I wish to hell we weren't out of cigarettes."

"So do I."

"We're going to make it, Ellen."

"Are we?"

"Our strength is as the strength of ten because our hearts are pure. But I wish we had a faster car. And a couple of machine guns in the back seat." His voice softened, the flipness suddenly gone. "We'll make it, Ellen. We'll make it."

Chapter 16

When they passed Castlemaine David braked the car at the summit of a rise on the eastern edge of the town. "Let's have a look," he said. "We can see the road a long way back from here. See anything?"

"No. Nothing that looks like—oh yes, I see him now. A long ways back. There are other cars with them. One could be Farrell's." She pointed it out. "We've got a good jump on them now."

"Good," he said. They got back into the car and started off again, and before long he had the Triumph up to its top speed once more.

The two cars, theirs and Koenig's, were fairly evenly matched. They had the advantage on curving roads, while Koenig had better speed up and down hills and on the straightaway. Once already he had closed the gap to less than a hundred yards, and the woman with him had drawn a pistol and snapped off a volley of shots at the Triumph. But the bullets hadn't come close.

David bent over the steering wheel. Ellen crouched low in her seat, her head cradled in her arms. David took a turn on two wheels, the tires screeching in protest, barreled out of the turn, and urged the car on. The Koenigs didn't make that turn. Ellen heard the screech of brakes applied too hard and too late, then the crashing of the heavy American car into the stone fence alongside the road.

David thought that the Koenigs' car might have been wrecked. "We can't stop to find out," he told her, "but I think they may be out of the play."

But later it seemed that they were still pursued. The accident had given them an extra few minutes, some of which they lost in Castlemaine when they stopped to buy cigarettes and fill the Triumph's gas tank. Since they didn't know how long the Koenig vehicle had been out of commission, it was hard to say whether they were widening the gap. It scarcely mattered. Koenig was very much on their trail, and it seemed likely that he had picked up reinforcements. They were alive and in the clear, but it was anybody's guess how long they would be able to hold their lead.

She drew on her cigarette. "There are plenty of roads that don't show up on the map," she said. "What would happen if we took one?"

"I don't know."

"Is it worth a try?"

"It may be, if we get desperate enough." He took the cigarette from her hand, took a puff, and gave it back to her. "But I'd rather stay on roads we know, so that we know where we're going. Some of the minor roads don't go anywhere, Ellen. They turn out to lead to some farmer's barn or wind up as dead ends. I'd hate to be on a dead-end road with Koenig and Farrell behind me."

"You're right."

She lapsed into silence, turning from time to time to gaze through the rear window at the road behind them. Another car had come up behind them since they left Castlemaine, a local car, not one of their pursuers, and the car effectively blocked her view of the road. She watched, and the car gradually drew abreast of them, honked its intention to pass, and swung easily out around them and raced on ahead. It was a low-slung sports car, a Jaguar, and it rushed on by as though they had been standing still in their tracks.

She released her breath and realized for the first time that she had been holding it. She shuddered.

"Something the matter?"

"The way that car passed us."

"You didn't think it was them, did you?"

"No, I knew it wasn't. Just the ease with which it got ahead of us. I wish we had a car like that."

"See any beggars riding?"

"I don't—oh, I see. Wishes aren't horses, are they? Let alone Jaguars."

"Uh-huh."

"At least they don't have a Jaguar either. They wouldn't have gone into the fence if they did, would they?"

"No. While you're wishing, you could wish we had a gun."

"I wouldn't know what to do with one if we did. Would you?"

"I used to be fairly good with a rifle. And I've fired handguns, though not very accurately. There isn't one in the back seat, is there?"

"I'll look."

There was nothing in the back seat.

"How about the trunk?"

"I saw the inside of the trunk when I put the blanket away.

I didn't notice anything inside, but I suppose it's possible. Do you want to stop the car and look?"

He shook his head. "Not very likely there'll be anything there. People who carry guns aren't apt to stow them in the trunk. I wish we had some sort of weapon. Next time I stop the car, remind me to get the tire iron from the trunk. It's better than nothing."

"Against a gun?"

"It's still better than nothing."

Then she remembered. "He said he had a knife, under the driver's seat. He told me all about the knife." She shivered again, involuntarily. "He may have been lying."

"Take a look."

She fumbled under his seat. Her hand touched something cold and metallic. She drew it out. It was just as Farrell had described it—a knife with a long, thin blade. She tested the edge with her thumb. It felt very sharp and looked deadly.

"A knife and a tire iron," she said. "Bit by bit, we're developing an arsenal."

"Put it in your purse."

They swung around another hairpin turn, and Ellen felt something slide out from under the seat and strike her foot. Looking down, she exclaimed, "David!" She reached down, and her fingers closed around a revolver.

"What luck!" said David. "Put that in your purse too. It won't fit in my pocket, I'm afraid."

She did as he said and was barely able to snap the purse shut over the revolver.

"That gun may come in handy," he said. "Let's just hope we don't have to use it."

*   *   *

When they crossed the boundary line into County Cork she thought of the other time she had crossed that same border, from Cork into Kerry. It had been a matter of days ago, and yet her world then had been entirely different from what it had since become. She remembered how she had roamed over this same countryside, her guitar over her shoulder, her eyes continually going wide in fascination at the beauty of the land and the charm of its people. Now she was seeing this same countryside for a second time, and its charm and beauty were quite lost to her. It had become transformed from a phenomenon in its own right to a backdrop for the drama of which she and David were a part.

How very different it had all been then. And what a different person she had been, concerned only with songs and their singers, busy recording songs and learning them and meeting people and enjoying life. Spies then had been creatures in books and movies, and death something that happened to the very old. She clutched her purse close and thought of what it contained, the sinister scrap of microfilm, the equally sinister knife. Tangible evidence of this new world inhabited by a new Ellen Cameron.

They drove to Newmarket, then took the northern branch of a fork leading to Freemount. The sky was clouded over now, the sun no longer in view. She wondered if it was going to rain. Rain would cut their top speed, but it would also lessen the speed of those in pursuit. She didn't know whether it would work out to their advantage.

She turned automatically to look out the rear window. No one in sight. She reported the fact to David, and he replied with a nod. His hands were tight on the wheel, his face drawn. He too was feeling the strain. She wondered how much more of it they could take. Sooner or later they would have to stop. They couldn't drive all night. And then what would happen? Where would they go?

They could stop in a town, she thought. If they drove straight to a gardai station, the police would give them protection. And if they picked one of the larger towns, they would have a good chance of finding police officers who would believe their story and understand the depths of their difficulties.

She opened the map and studied it intently. Tipperary City seemed to fit the requirements. It was large enough to boast a sizable police force, and it could be reached by back roads that would give them an advantage over the fast cars behind them.

She told David her idea.

"I don't know," he said.

"How long can we keep running?"

"That's a point, but I hate to stop. Once we stop, they catch up with us."

"But the police . . ."

"The gardai might have a little trouble believing our story. And I don't know how well they can protect us. Farrell strikes me as a fairly daring man, Ellen. I don't think he'd draw the line at shooting his way into a police station if he had to."

She drew a breath. "Then you don't want to stop at Tipperary?"

"We'll see. It might be a good idea after all. And maybe we'll get lucky and shake them off our trail by then. If we don't . . ."

"Then what?"

"Then maybe we'll stop."

The little car rolled on. She kept looking back to check, and she didn't see any car she could recognize as Koenig's.

The road grew curvier, and the rain, a threat for some time, became a reality. It came down hard and fast, and the little car's windshield wipers struggled to keep up with it.

"How's the driving?"

"Bad."

"Very bad?"

"Rotten visibility, and the road surface is slippery. It'll be a little better in fifteen minutes or so. When it first starts to rain, the water piles up on the accumulated oil slick on the highway surface. After it's been raining awhile, the oil washes away. It's still worse than dry pavement, but not as bad as it is now."

"Do you think we should slow down?"

"I don't dare."

"David . . ."

And then it happened all at once, far too quickly for her to realize what was going on. They came around a blind curve, the throttle wide open, and suddenly the road in front of them was filled with sheep. A farmer, crooked stick in hand, dog at heels, was leading his sheep across into another field, and she stared at the sea of wooly white creatures and shouted *"David, look out,"* and felt the brakes grab and the car careen wildly out of control.

The impact was terrible. The car plowed into the middle of the flock, scattering bits of sheep in all directions, spinning out of control, almost tipping over on its side, then coming to a sudden violent stop.

They got out of the car. The farmer could not pay any attention to them at first. He was on his knees in the middle of the mass of torn and bleeding animals, his own voice as shrill and strained as the awful bleating of the sheep. Sobbing, he moved among them. He took a jackknife from his pocket and opened it, and he moved among the mass of woolly forms, talking to them gently, sadly, and using the knife to cut the throats of the hopelessly crippled beasts, putting an end to their misery.

She had never seen such carnage. She clutched David's arm, certain that she was going to be sick, fighting off wave after wave of nausea. She looked at their own car, crippled like the sheep, its front shoved in through the radiator, steam or smoke pouring forth from under the hood. The sheep would never walk again and the car would never be driven again, and she clung to David's arm and closed her eyes as the world swayed around her.

The man was saying, "Oh, my beauties, my pets. Ah, my poor beauties. Six, seven of them, gone, gone."

From the east a motorcycle came into view, its engine audible over the bleating of the surviving sheep, which were milling about in terror, filling the road. The motorcycle screeched to a stop. A rural policeman, his uniform a rich forest green, the visor of his cap shining brilliantly, stepped down from the cycle.

And far off to the west she heard, or thought she heard, the engines of approaching cars. Farrell and the Koenigs, coming their way.

Chapter 17

The policeman was very understanding, very sympathetic, and very efficient. He comforted the shepherd, who had by now become somewhat more resigned to the fate of the unfortunate animals. And he spoke easily to David, first reminding him of the dangers of driving too fast over unfamiliar roads, then explaining that since they were tourists in a strange land, and since the government of the Republic of Ireland wished to make life as simple as possible for tourists, they might resolve the affair with a minimum of red tape.

"I'll need a look at your driving licenses and vehicular registration," he said. "And your passports, too, if you've them with you. And then if Mr. Mahoney can estimate the value of the slain animals, and if the sum's one you won't object to paying out of pocket, then we'll be after fixing this up with no trouble. There's a garage in the next town over that can make repairs to your auto. I see it's an Irish registration—is it a rented car? For perhaps you can call the rental agency and they'll arrange another car for you, though you'll no doubt be staying overnight. You needn't worry about the car, they all carry insurance on them . . ."

But they had a great deal to worry about. They did not have registration papers for the automobile, nor did they have enough money to pay for the sheep. How much, she wondered, was a sheep worth? What was adequate compensation for a half dozen dumb animals torn to pieces by a car?

She shuddered. Their car was crippled, immobile. A policeman had them at hand and would not allow them to escape. And a car was after them, one car and probably two, and with every passing second their lead was being reduced. At any moment the large American car might come into view. She knew what would happen then. The policeman would be no protection for them. Koenig's first shots would fell the sturdy garda in his tracks. Another bullet would leave the heartsick shepherd as dead as his lamented sheep. And other bullets would tear into her and David.

David was saying, "You'd better get your purse, dear. You have the registration papers."

"But I don't—"

His eyes locked with hers; one closed briefly in a conspiratorial wink. "The papers," he said. "In your purse."

He wanted her to get her purse from the car. But why? She didn't bother searching for an answer to the question. There was no time. Cars in the distance, behind them—yes, it would be Koenig, Koenig and Farrell, and they would come hurtling round the curve . . .

She opened the door on the passenger side of the car and picked up her purse from the seat. David was talking to the policeman. She could not hear what they were saying. Her eyes took in the entire scene. The shepherd and his dogs leading the last of the frightened sheep over to the side of the road and through the gap in the fence to the field beyond. The policeman talking with David. The motorcycle, resting on its standard, neat and trim and efficient in appearance as the man who rode it. And the bodies of the seven dead sheep, all white wool and red blood.

When she approached the men, her purse in her hand, David looked at her. "Mr. Mahoney says that he'll be satisfied with seven pounds ten each for the sheep, Ellen. There were seven of them, so that comes to, let me see, fifty-two pounds and ten, which is what? Fifty pounds is one hundred forty dollars, plus two pounds is another five-sixty, and ten shillings is a dollar-forty. That comes to what?"

The policeman shook his head.

David said, "One hundred forty-seven dollars, so if you'll give Mr. Mahoney an even hundred and fifty that should be good all around. And we'll need the registration papers for the car. Check your purse and see if you can find everything, if you're not too nervous."

Bewildered, she made a show of opening her purse and checking its contents. The pistol, which she had momentarily forgotten, lay wickedly in her purse. Was that what he wanted?

"Having trouble, dear?"

The cars were coming closer; she could hear them clearly now, two of them, with the powerful rumble characteristic of American engines and instantly identifiable on a quiet Irish lane. "See if you can find everything, if you're not too nervous," he had said. Was that her cue? And he was walking to her side now to join her . . .

She raised her head apologetically. "I'm so sorry," she said, "but I'm such a muddle, I can't see straight. I'm so shaken. David, will you look for me?"

He took the purse from her. The shepherd, anxious now to be paid for his dead sheep, was at David's side. In a flash

David had an arm around the little old man. His free hand held the gun pointed at the policeman.

"Nobody move," he snapped. To the garda he said, "Raise your hands and keep them high. Don't make a move."

"You're after making a mistake, lad," the garda said. "You'll save fifty pounds and buy a world of trouble. Put the gun down."

"Ellen, move over by the motorcycle."

"First be thinking, girl."

"Ellen—"

The cars. She went to the motorcycle.

David released the shepherd and told him to run off with his sheep. The man was plainly terrified.

David waved the gun at him. "Run!"

The shepherd ran.

David said, "There's no time. You—get over by the side of the road. Stand out of the way. Ellen, keep this pointed at him." She took the gun and aimed it at the policeman, knowing that she could do nothing if he tried to take it away from her, that she could not bring herself to shoot him in a million years. It was all bluff—but as long as the policeman didn't know it was bluff, it didn't matter.

And the policeman wasn't sure enough to make his move. He stood at the roadside, his hands in the air, waiting.

Ellen was terrified, and she was ashamed of what she and David had to do, but she was at this moment grateful that policemen in Ireland, like those in England, carried no guns.

David was astride the cycle. He kicked off the stand, got the engine started. "Give me the gun." She gave it to him, and he jammed it down beneath the waistband of his trousers. "Now get on behind me. Lock your arms around my waist.

And take hold of the purse, you've got to hang on to it, because I have to drive. Hold on as tight as you can . . ."

The cars. She heard the lead auto now, Koenig's, coming around the bend. She heard the squeal of brakes as the heavy car pulled to a jolting stop inches from the torn bodies of the dead sheep.

Then the motorcycle leaped forward, shaking and bucking like an unbroken stallion, and she held on to David for dear life.

Chapter 18

It was a shaking, bone-jolting ride. The motorcycle's top speed was slightly higher than that of the Triumph but seemed to Ellen at least three times as fast. She rode with her arms locked tightly around David's middle and her face pressed up against the back of his bulky sweater. The wind, cold and rain-laden, played furiously with her hair. Rain was everywhere, soaking into her clothes and wetting her to the skin, splashing up at her from puddles in the road.

At first she had been certain that they would be caught. Koenig had never come so close before, and only the dead sheep on the road had saved them. Koenig had had to brake hard, his attention fastened on stopping the huge car safely, and before he could settle himself and send bullets their way they were off, the motorcycle leaping beneath them, plunging headlong down the road.

She was wrapped in wind and rain and noise, the constant roar of the cycle, the whining of the wind in her ear. There were things she wanted to say to David, questions she had to ask him, but conversation was presently impossible. Once, she tried to shout to him, but he failed to hear her over the combined roar of motorcycle and wind. She gave up the attempt and held on to him for dear life.

She could barely believe what had happened, and her own

feelings were hopelessly confused. On the one hand she was overcome with admiration for David. He had acted so quickly, so precisely, sending her for her purse, taking it from her, then using the gun to force the policeman to surrender his motorcycle. Another moment's delay and they would have been finished, and the shepherd and policeman killed in the bargain. But now, at least for the time being, they were free.

And at the same time she was afraid, terribly afraid, of what they had done. They had stolen an Irish policeman's motorcycle. Their earlier plan, one of seeking refuge with the police at Tipperary, was no longer workable. A single act had transformed the police from friends to enemies, at least until they could straighten things out. They had to run, not only from Koenig and Farrell and their gang, but from the police as well. Before, they had been fugitives from evil; now they were fugitives from the law, too.

She pressed her face into the comforting warmth of David's sweater. Her eyes glanced down at the road surface below as it flew by beneath the wheels of the motorcycle. She had never been on a motorcycle before, had always been scared to take a ride. It did not frighten her now—as though there were no room within her for additional fear, as though she already had as much fear in her as she could manage at one time.

Koenig and Farrell could be behind them right now, she thought. They could have caught up, they could be bearing down on the motorcycle at any moment and she would never know it. She could not turn around to look behind her. Surely the carnage in the roadway would have delayed them for a while, but not for very long. And it was impossible for her to estimate how fast the motorcycle was going. She couldn't see the speedometer from where she sat, and although it felt to her as though they were exceeding the speed of sound, she knew they were probably making less speed than a fast car was capable of.

Without warning, tears welled up behind her eyes and spilled onto her cheeks. She was not sobbing; the tears simply flowed of their own accord, fighting her attempts to blink them back. She tightened her grip around David's body, clinging to him, her eyes tightly shut, her teeth clenched hard together.

She wished, not for the first time, that she could pray . . . .

When finally he braked the motorcycle to a gradual stop she loosened her grip around his waist and dismounted. He lowered the kickstand and stepped away from the motorcycle. There were no cars approaching from either direction. She found her cigarettes in her purse. She gave one to him and kept one for herself, and he lit them both, cupping the match in his hand to shield the flame from wind and rain.

She said, "Where are we?"

"Two miles outside of Mitchelstown, according to the sign.

"In Tipperary?"

"In Cork, but close to the county line. I don't dare drive into Mitchelstown. That garda must have got to a phone by now, and they'll be waiting for us. And we can't stay on the road any longer because they'll come looking for us."

"What are we going to do?"

"I don't know." He took his cigarette from his lips and looked at it. The rain had put it out. He shook his head and threw the cigarette off to the side of the road. "We made very good time. The motorcycle was flying."

"It felt that way."

"So we should have a good jump on Farrell and Koenig. But where do we go from here?"

"Do you think we might have lost them?"

"We could have, on any other road in the world. But this damned thing didn't have a single side road branching off ever since we got on the motorcycle. They could follow us with their eyes closed. There was just the one road, and we stayed with it, and so will they." He sighed. "Maybe I made a mistake. Maybe we shouldn't have taken the motorcycle, maybe we should have stayed there."

"We'd have been killed."

"That's what I figured. You know, if he tried to stop them, they might have shot him. But I don't think he would. Unless—"

"Unless what?"

"He may have asked them to give him a ride after us. And they may have refused, or else they may have taken the easiest way of refusal. By putting a bullet in him." He shook his head. "Poor man. He was very decent with us, made it very easy for us to pay for the sheep and cut through all sorts of red tape. And the price for the sheep certainly seemed reasonable enough. Though I don't honestly have any idea what a sheep's worth. Still, it *seemed* reasonable, didn't it?"

She nodded. She could still hear the horrible sounds of the dying sheep and the sounds Mr. Mahoney had made as he ended their suffering.

"They'd never have been so easy with us if the same thing happened in the States. So we return the favor by taking his motorcycle away from him. I wonder who's going to catch us first, the law or Farrell."

"Isn't there anywhere we can go?"

"There must be, but I can't think of it. Maybe we can hide the motorcycle and work our way into Mitchelstown on foot. Find someone there to hide us from Farrell and the police. But how do you walk up to someone out of the blue and tell him you've got a gang of spies after you, and the police as well? A man would have to be mad to take us in. More likely he'd hold a gun on us and call the gardai."

But she was only half-listening to him. There was something she remembered, something that had struck a responsive chord somewhere inside her. Something, a place to hide . . . .

"They're used to hiding men on the run. On the run from the British or from the Irish forces during the Civil War. But would they hide strangers? And strangers from overseas? Somebody might, but we don't know anyone. You didn't happen to pass through this part of the country on your way to Tralee?"

"No, I went south of here. I was in Cork City, so I took the southern route over. David . . ."

"If we only knew someone."

"David—Mitchelstown Caves!"

He looked blank.

"In the song," she said. "One of the verses to 'The Croppy Boy.' It's not in the standard versions, they all take place in Wexford, but there's one that I heard this trip where one of the croppy boys is a Tipperary boy who hides in the Mitchelstown caves. Oh, how does it go?"

She sang,

When we were beaten at Vinegar Hill
And the Saxon victors did burn and kill
Then I did fly straight to Mitchelstown
And in one damp cavern did I lay me down

And it's in this cavern dark I lie today
And pray no Saxon shall pass this way
Or from the scaffold at old Mountjoy
They'll hang the body of the Croppy Boy

"An old woman taught me the song," she said. "The caves are in Tipperary, a few miles northeast from Mitchelstown."

"Do you think we could find them?"

"Why not?"

He considered this. "It just might work. 'One damp cavern,' eh? It can't be much damper than I am already. We'd have to go on foot, and if it's five miles from Mitchelstown we've got an hour of walking ahead of us at the very least. It may be fairly dark by then, I don't know. Do you feel up to it?"

"I think so. We certainly can't stay here."

"No, we can't. We can't even walk on the road. We'll have to cut cross-country. We'd better get rid of the motorcycle. I wish there were a break in the fence. The thing's a perfect tipoff; anyone seeing it will know we've quit the road and started hiking."

"Can we lift it over?"

"Far too heavy. Give me a hand." They wheeled the machine off to the side of the road and propped it against the fence. David got the knife from her purse and climbed over the fence, hacking at some of the shrubbery. He passed branches over the fence to her and she arranged them upon the motorcycle, piling them up to obscure it from view. He climbed back over the fence and examined the motorcycle under its pile of camouflage.

"To me," he said, "it looks like a motorcycle with branches piled on it."

"But if they come roaring by at sixty miles an hour . . ."

"That's a thought. I don't know, it might work. Let's get off the road, Ellen. We'll want to cut this way" —he pointed— "and just walk until we come to something that looks like a cave, I guess. I don't know. How are you feeling?"

"All right."

"Cold and wet and miserable?"

"A little of each, I suppose. But I'll manage."

"And hungry?"

"I was hoping you wouldn't mention it. I've been trying not to think about it."

"Sorry."

"It's all right. I'm tired, too, as far as that goes. And soaked and scared. I'll feel better when we get far enough from the road so that they won't be able to see us. I hope that cave's there. And that we'll come somewhere close to it."

By the time they reached the cave she had long ago given up hope of ever finding it. She was walking on sheer momentum and running low of that. Before, she had been cold and wet and miserable and hungry and tired and afraid. Now she was all these things to an even greater extent. The ground over which they had been walking was spongy with rain. Her shoes were soaked through and her feet were chilled to the bone. Walking had grown progressively more arduous. The muscles in her calves knotted up, and for a time every step was agony. Then it grew easier; either the knots had worked out of the muscles or she was too numb to notice them.

They walked on, they blundered around, they climbed over ditches and banks and unmortared stone fences. The twilight grew dimmer and the darkness came on, and the rain did not let up or the wind abate. Several times she felt at the point of collapse. She was sure they would drop in a field, only to awaken chilled and feverish at dawn. But they walked on. David held her when she was weak and comforted her when her fear threatened to rage out of control, and because he was there she was able to go on.

When they found the cave, when it turned out to be right where it was supposed to be, when it loomed before them like a whale's mouth, she thought at first that it could only be a mirage. Just as men saw water in the desert, she and David were seeing a cave in the middle of the waterlogged hilly meadows of Tipperary. But it was no mirage. They hurried to the cave and found shelter inside it.

It was dark, and they had no flashlight. David lit matches to illuminate the cave's interior. It was large, larger than the inside of Gallarus Oratory, and extended back much farther, with labyrinthine passages working far back into the side of a hill. Whether it was damp she could not say. She was too wet herself to know.

David was kneeling at the rear. "There have been people here," he said. "See? The remains of a campfire here, and dry wood stacked against the wall for another fire. I wish I knew how recent the fire was. It could have been made a day ago or many years ago. There's probably a way to tell, but I don't know it."

"Maybe it was the croppy boy's."

"Could be. Should I build a fire?"

"I don't know. If they could see it . . ."

"Go outside for a minute," he said. "I'll light a match and hold it around. Let me know if you can see it."

She went to the mouth of the cave and stepped outside.

"Anything?"

"I can't see a thing."

"Good," he said. "Come on back."

She went to him. He was gathering firewood from the pile at the side of the cave, shaving down a few sticks with the long knife to make kindling. He worked quickly, whittling a pile of scraps that would catch a flame and give a start to the larger branches and logs.

"What about the smoke?"

"There's a fissure overhead," he said. "A break in the rock. It should serve as a natural chimney. Besides, this wood is bone dry. It's been here a long time, and it shouldn't throw much smoke at all." He shrugged. "I suppose it's chancy, but it's a chance we pretty much have to take. We'll be able to dry our clothes and warm ourselves. I don't know about you, but if I don't thaw out soon I'm going to turn blue. And you look in pretty sad shape yourself."

"I have had better days."

"Uh-huh."

He scratched a match and used its light to arrange the kindling in a neat ball upon the ashes of the former campfire. Then he positioned thinner sticks over the ball of kindling, making a tent-shaped arrangement. He set up a neat square of larger pieces of wood around the little tent, then scratched another match and applied it to the kindling. In just a few minutes a small fire was burning brightly, casting a warm glow around the interior of the cave.

"You must have been a Boy Scout."

"Uh-huh."

"I think you qualify for a fire-building merit badge. Is there such a thing?"

"I don't know. But I'm a man of many talents. Wait a minute—I want to see if the fire shows at all from the outside."

He was back seconds later, reporting that it was quite invisible. "And it's getting darker and darker now," he said. "They'll probably quit for the night. I think we're safe, croppy girl. You found us a good place to hide."

"It was just luck that I remembered it. And that we found it. I was beginning to think I had sent us all around Robin Hood's barn, but we're here, aren't we?"

"That we are." He straightened up. "I'll, uh, go sit by the entranceway and keep watch. You'd better get out of those clothes and dry them over the fire. Not too close, or they'll raise too much smoke. But get out of them for now, that's the main thing."

He was on his way before she could object. She felt odd, undressing in the campfire light, and as she stepped out of her underthings she was conscious of David sitting in darkness near the mouth of the cave. He could turn around and see her and she would not know the difference.

The thought made her giggle and blush at the same time. What earthly difference, she wondered, could it possibly make? Another Ellen Cameron would have been quite nervous at the thought of being undressed in the presence of a man. But that earlier Ellen Cameron no longer existed. She had passed away forever in the course of their escape, and the girl who had taken her place was made of sterner stuff.

She placed her clothing on the bare earth by the side of the fire. David, she thought, was carrying chivalry beyond the bounds of good sense. He was as cold and wet and miserable as she, but an excess of gentlemanliness was leaving him at the front of the cave while she dried and warmed herself. She thought of summoning him back, then decided to wait, at least until her underthings were dry. They were all nylon and would dry quickly.

When they had dried she put them on and called him back. He stopped halfway to the fire and offered to wait until she was dressed.

"Oh, don't be silly," she said. "First things first. Besides, I think we know each other well enough to forget propriety a little."

"Of course, but if it bothers you . . ."

"It doesn't."

She noticed, though, how he avoided looking directly at her. She moved past him to the front of the cave. Later he called her back. He was dressed again, except for his trousers and socks. She put on her skirt and blouse and sat beside him and gazed into the fire. Like the sea, it exerted a definite hypnotic effect on her.

"Tired, Ellen?"

"A little. I don't think I could sleep, though."

"Why not try? I'll keep watch."

"Oh, I don't—"

"Just lie down and relax, then. I won't let you sleep long. Don't worry. But it'll be good for you to get a little rest."

"How about you?"

"If I get sleepy, I'll wake you and let you stand watch. Fair enough?"

"I guess so, but . . ."

"Go ahead."

She stretched out on the hard ground, her eyes still fixed upon the fire. She let her mind wander, let her thoughts stray far and wide. Her eyes closed of their own accord, and sleep took her by surprise.

All at once he was shaking her awake. She tried to fight him off, tried to slip back under the protective cloak of sleep, but he wouldn't let her. Then she opened her mouth to cry out but his hand fastened over it.

"Shhhh," he cautioned. "They're outside."

Her eyes widened, and she clutched his arm in fear.

"About a dozen of them," he said. "They have flashlights and guns. I haven't seen any uniforms. They're about a hundred yards away, spread out over the sides of the hills. I think it must be Farrell's gang. The police wouldn't have to be so silent about it. Are you feeling all right, Ellen?"

"I guess so. Are they going to . . . to find us?"

"I don't know. Why don't you come up front and have a look? Maybe you'll recognize them."

She peered out from the cave's entrance. At first she saw only shapes and lights, but then her eyes focused and she was able to make out the faces of the men. She recognized Farrell and Koenig and the thin man who had mugged her in London and tracked her in Cork. She was surprised how strangely calm she felt now. They had been running for so long, knowing only that their pursuers were at their backs. Now at least the crisis was approaching, and there was something comforting in the knowledge. They were in more danger now than they had ever been. But at least they did not have to run. At least they knew who was after them and where they were.

She crawled back into the rear of the cavern. "It's Farrell and Koenig," she whispered. "I recognized them. How do you suppose they found us?"

"They must have spotted the motorcycle."

"But we walked for miles . . ."

He nodded. "And probably left a trail a yard wide," he said. "Remember, they have lights. And we were in a hurry. I guess they didn't have much trouble following us."

"Do they know we're in this cave?"

"I don't think so. But they know we're in one of the caves around here, and they'll get to this one in a matter of time." He was carefully scattering the campfire, beating out the little tongues of flame with his sweater. Then he picked up the gun.

"What are you going to do?"

"Nothing yet. But we're in a good position for defense. They can't rush us, the cave's mouth is too narrow. We may be able to hold out."

"How many bullets do you have?"

"Half a dozen. But they don't know that."

"And when morning comes? When it's light out?"

"We'll worry about that when the time comes."

He moved toward the mouth of the cave, and she followed after him. They crouched in the darkness, off to the side. She watched men moving cautiously, playing their powerful flash-lights back and forth over the terrain. Koenig drew a revolver from a shoulder holster, pointed it off to the left. She steeled herself, and when the gunshot sounded she did not utter a sound. The shot was to scare them, she knew; Koenig hoped they would cry out at the noise, or shoot back, thus revealing themselves.

One man was headed their way. Ellen looked at him, trying to remember if she had seen him before. He looked familiar, but she could not be certain. He moved ever closer to the mouth of the cave, and his flashlight shone into the cavern, illuminating the dark walls.

He called out, "I think it's this one!" A Scot, she guessed, by his accent. And he put one foot into the cave and swung his light their way, and David shot him in the throat.

Blood poured from the wound, a red river staining the cavern floor. David grabbed the dead man and pulled him inside. He snatched up the flashlight and tore an automatic pistol from the corpse's grasp. Ellen pressed flat against the wall. Some shots rang out from the field. David snapped off a quick shot in return, and the men outside dropped behind cover.

"We've got a stalemate," she heard David say softly. "They've got us bottled up and we can't get out. But they can't get in, either."

"Now what happens?"

"We wait."

For a long moment nothing at all happened. She stared at the dead man, saw the barren stare in his eyes, the pool of drying blood. He looked unreal, as if he had never been alive at all. She looked at him and thought of the dead sheep in the roadway.

They had two guns now, she thought. And the dead man had never fired his pistol, so it probably had a full load. How many shots did that mean? Six? Not all guns were six-shooters, she knew. She wanted to ask David how many bullets the gun held, but she did not want to break the silence, so she said nothing.

Perhaps six bullets. And David had fired twice, so that left four in the revolver.

Ten shots.

"David Clare!" It was Farrell, bellowing across the field, his voice shattering the silence of the night. "Good shooting, Clare!"

They said nothing.

"But do you always shoot that well? And how many shots do you have left?"

"Find out for yourself, Father."

The false priest roared with laughter. "Come on out here," he called. "Surrender and we'll let you live. The whole thing's shot now anyway, Clare. All I'm interested in is the film. Give us that and we'll let you go."

"*Sure* you will."

"Why not? Killing bores me, Clare."

David didn't answer this time. She saw his hand tighten on the grip of the revolver, saw the lines of tension in his face.

"Clare! Our little girl thought you were the killer. Did she tell you?"

"She told me."

"Funny, isn't it? And now you're going to die trying to save her. A girl who wouldn't trust you an inch, and you're going to die at her side."

"We're neither of us dead yet, Father."

There was a pause. Then a volley of shots rang out, peppering the floor and the walls of the cave but none of them coming close to her or David. "They can't get to us," he told her. "They can waste bullets, but they can't get to us."

"Clare! You think you're sitting pretty, don't you?"

"I think so."

"How long will you last without sleep? Or food? Or water?"

"We've got food and water. And we can last a long time without sleep, Father."

"Brave talk. You can make a deal. Throw out the film."

"You're too late."

"What do you mean?"

"We already burned it, Father. And the passport. So you might as well collect your boys and go home."

There was a pause. "You're a liar."

"So are you," David shouted back. "Now cut the games. You want the film, and the passport, and us, you come get them. No deals."

"We'll starve you out."

"Maybe."

"Or we'll hurry things up with tear gas."

"If you had tear gas you'd have used it already. Forget it."

Another roar of laughter. Farrell was insane, she realized. Absolutely insane. Even now, temporarily frustrated, he was enjoying himself immensely. It was all life and death, but he was happy as a child with a new toy. It was all a game to him.

"We'll get you when the sun comes up, Clare. We'll have you trapped then, and we'll be able to see."

"So will I. You want to lead the pack, Father? I never shot a priest before."

More laughter. More shots sounded out, but fewer this time. Again the bullets were all wide of the mark.

"David?" Her voice was a whisper. "Do we have a chance?"

"I don't know."

"You sounded so sure of yourself."

"He wants us to beg. I won't give him the satisfaction."

"What he said . . ." She didn't want to ask the questions but forced herself. "Will they be able to starve us out? Or will we fall asleep after a long enough wait?"

"Maybe."

"David . . ."

"They can't stand out there with their guns forever. Someone has to pass by sooner or later. The longer we hold out, the longer we stay awake and alert, the better a chance we have."

She nodded, her teeth clenched. How very brave he was, she thought. He had managed such a confident air of defiance with Farrell, shouting at the false priest with assurance in his voice. And all the while he had known that the situation was virtually hopeless—

"Make sure the fire is going," he said suddenly. "Hug the wall and go back to it. I scattered it somewhat, but it should be burning. Add a little more wood to it."

"Why?"

"If we have to give up, I want the passport burned. And their precious microfilm. I don't want them to have it."

She swallowed. She was going to cry now, she knew it, she couldn't help it. But she swallowed, and the tears stayed back.

She said, "Shall I burn them now?"

"No."

"In case there's no time . . ."

"No." He took her hand. "If we get out of this alive, we'll want to be able to turn that film over to the right people. Besides . . ." He laughed, and for the first time in her life she knew what *gallows humor* really meant. "And besides, they'll never let you back into the States if you lose your passport."

*   *   *

When the noise first came from deep in the rear of the cave, she thought it was some small animal burrowing around there. But the noise came closer, slowly closer, and she could tell that it was a man making his way into the cavern. She huddled close to David, and he turned to cover the rear of the cave with his pistol.

"If there's a back entrance . . ."

"We can still cover it," he said.

"Can we?"

There was a dry cough behind them, out of sight. The cough was repeated. "Hold your fire," a soft voice said. The words barely carried to the front of the cave.

And then, from the darkness, a man emerged. He was not more than an inch or two over five feet tall, and his old face was deeply lined with wrinkles. Black hair peppered with gray stuck out from beneath a ragged cloth cap. He wore an ancient tweed jacket that reached almost to his knees, and in one hand he held an odd sort of gun, larger than a pistol, smaller than a rifle.

"Ah," he said, his voice no more than a whisper. "Sure, and it's a fair Donnybrook, by the sound of it. What, and only two of you, and such a lot of them outside?" He shook his head sadly. "I thought it could be some of the boys, but ye aren't faces I know, nor Irish by the look of ye. And if I'm not prying, could you be after telling me the nature of the row?"

Chapter 19

The gnarled little old man did not demand details. The bare outline of their story, told by David in a hushed whisper, was enough to redden the old man's face with righteous fury. "Sure, and they're the very spawn of hell," he said. "And masquerading as a priest in the bargain. Faith, Patrick drove the snakes out of Ireland and now they're after coming back!"

"Can you get us out?"

"I could."

"Will you?"

"I will, but they'll only be coming after you. That such children of the devil should be in Ireland! In Tipperary!"

"What can we do?"

The man's eyes twinkled, and he instantly looked years younger. "Tell me," he demanded, "could you hold out for another hour?"

"Easily."

"And would you live to see these jackeens get their due?"

"How?"

"Why, I'll call some of the boys around. They'll be sleeping, but our boys wake easy. And every man has a gun, and some more than guns. They've all the odds on their side now, but we can even the odds a wee bit."

David said. "Those are professional assassins out there. They're probably all good shots and used to this sort of thing."

"Oh, and is it professionals they are!" The little man drew himself straight up and puffed out his chest. "And are our boys such amateurs? And wasn't I in Barry's column myself, and in on the fun at Macroom? And wasn't young Fergal O'Hara up fighting in the Six Counties ten years ago, and him only twenty-six years old this month? And didn't Seamus Finn blow up half of Liverpool in 1940 with a bit of gel-ignite and an old alarm clock? Ah, it's not such amateurs the boys are, lad. We've no uniforms and no aircraft, but we're the Irish Republican Army, and if the rascals want a fight they'll be after having one soon enough. We beat the Tans and we fought the Free Staters and we'll be fighting in the North if we have to, and if such filth as them can shoot straight and fast, why, we can shoot twice as straight and twice as fast. And with Mauser pistols and Sten guns and such as will make their weaponry nothing at all. Professionals they are, are they? And in an hour's time they'll be so that they'll never practice their profession again, not this side of hell. You wait here for me. Take my Mauser pistol, give them a spraying now and then. And I'll be with you in an hour's time, and may God wither my right arm if Mick O'Sullivan ever dodged a fight if it was a right one."

He was back in considerably less than an hour. They heard him moving quickly but quietly at the rear of the cave, and then he coughed his dry warning cough, paused, coughed again. Then he appeared in the firelight. There was another gun in his hand, larger than the Mauser pistol, and his worn cloth cap was pitched at a rakish angle.

"I gathered up eight of the boys," Mick O'Sullivan said. "Eight good boys, and Paddy Dugan was after coming too, but his heart's been troubling him and I told him we had plenty of men. Now keep a good ear open, lad. The boys are taking their positions now, and Seamus Finn's down on the road, slashing their tires so that they won't be making their escape in their autos. Listen for the hoot of an owl, then a pause, and then the hooting again. That means that everyone's where he ought to be, behind the hedgerows and the thickets, guns and spotlights at the ready."

"Will eight men be enough?"

"When it's our boys," O'Sullivan said, "three would be enough. But how could I let the others miss out on the fun, and all of them lads I've known for years?"

They waited, silent now. Then they heard the hooting of an owl, and silence, and the hoot repeated.

"The boys are ready," O'Sullivan said. "And it's for me to give the signal." He flattened out on the floor of the cave, inched forward, his Sten gun out in front of him, his finger on the trigger. "Stand clear," he advised, "but you'll want to watch the show. The Molotov cocktails first, to give us some light to fire by. And to shake up these 'professionals' of yours. A bit of flame does that, you know. Scares them so that they don't know where to shoot first."

O'Sullivan inched forward. There was a moment of utter silence, and then his thin old voice rang out over the countryside like a bugle.

"Up the Republic!"
And the slaughter began.

It was no battle. It was a rout, a massacre. The instant O'Sullivan's cry broke the stillness of the night, the fields erupted in violence. The bottles of gasoline came first, showering over ditches and hedgerows with bitter accuracy, exploding, brightening the fields with flames. Then shots rang out—the chatter of automatic weapons, the deadly blasts of rifles and handguns. Mills bombs, homemade canisters of destruction, hurtled down on Farrell and his men.

A man—the thin-faced man, the mugger from London— rose screaming and ran into the night, his clothes in flames. O'Sullivan fingered the Sten gun's trigger and sent a stream of bullets climbing the man's back from his belt to his head. The scream died in a throaty gasp and a thin man sprawled dead on the ground, his clothing still flaming.

From all corners of the field the shooting went on, a furious barrage of destruction. Farrell's men were firing back but did not know where to shoot or what to shoot at. One was on his feet, his hands high over his head, shrieking that he surrendered. A Mills bomb arced through the air and landed at his feet. He looked at it, hypnotized, still screaming, then tried to back away. The bomb blew off both his legs.

"Surrender," O'Sullivan said scornfully. "They'll be prisoners of war, will they? The fires of hell they will."

There would be no surrenders, no prisoners. Ellen watched, transfixed, as the merciless destruction continued. She saw a heavyset man break into a run, watched as gunmen on all sides picked him up as a target. It was Koenig. Bullets tore at his legs, his body. They ripped into him from all directions, and he seemed to be dancing like a puppet on strings, miraculously staying on his feet.

"And why are they wasting bullets?" O'Sullivan demanded. "It's only the gunfire that's keeping him on his feet. He's been long dead, he has." As he spoke the words, Koenig toppled and fell.

A high-pitched scream. Another figure broke cover and ran toward the road. Again the guns spoke, and as they found their mark Ellen saw that it was a woman. Koenig's woman.

"That there should be a woman in such business," O'Sullivan said. "Who would have thought I'd see the day that I'd be shooting women? Or that I'd see the day that women came into the fields with guns."

Gradually the staccato of gunfire died down. Flashlights played carefully over the terrain. Men in long jackets and caps came into view, moving through the battlefield, making certain that none of the spy gang were still alive. Ellen heard soft moaning off to the left and saw a young Irish boy walk over to the source of the moaning. His flashlight revealed a man on his back, blood pouring from a wound in his side, his head cradled in his arms. The boy put his pistol to the back of the wounded man's head and blew his brains out.

And Mick O'Sullivan said, "You'll come out and meet the boys now. And have a look at these 'professionals,' such as they were. Eight of us, and did you ask if eight would be enough! Two of us could have done the job and done it right. Professionals!"

*   *   *

David held her arm. They walked back and forth over the fields, studying the wrecked bodies of the men who had planned to kill them. They found Koenig and his woman and the long thin man, but they did not find Farrell. His body did not turn up.

"He never escaped," O'Sullivan insisted. "No man escaped. But one of the bombs could have taken him, and there'd be too little left in one piece to know it was him. There's none of them escaped, and ye may count on it."

Ellen swayed. It was over, they were going to live, they were all right now . . .

"Ye'll meet the boys. Ellen Cameron and David Clare they are, and here are Seamus Finn who slashed their tires, and Fergal O'Hara. And here's my own son Sean, and a good boy he is. And Jimmy Davis" —he pointed to the boy who had blown out the brains of the wounded man— "and just seventeen he is, and never fired a pistol at a man before to-night, and how well he did I'll not soon forget." Jimmy Davis glowed with pride. "And Tom Behan and Sean Cassidy and Peader Killeen. And now we'll go round to Fergal's house. You'll be hungry, not eating the whole day and night, and you look to be needing a touch of poteen. And the boys will have a taste from the jar, I know."

There was laughter from the men.

"We'll be after having a hooley," O'Sullivan said. "Fergal's mother has the food cooking for ye already, and the jars out on the table. It's a victory celebration, do ye know."

She couldn't help it. She had held it back too long, and now there was no need to fight it any longer, no need at all. Her legs sagged and her shoulders heaved and she collapsed against David, fell into his arms, crying and crying, crying like a baby. It was all over and there was nothing to worry about and she couldn't stop crying to save her soul.

The men turned away, embarrassed. And David held her, firmly but gently, held her tight in his arms until the crying stopped.

Chapter 20

Fergal O'Hara and his widowed mother lived in a tiny cottage with a thatched roof upon which an anachronistic television antenna was perched. The main room of the cottage was crowded now with the eight "boys" and Ellen and David. Mrs. O'Hara, a thin little woman with snow-white hair and cool blue eyes, kept bringing food from the kitchen. Lamb chops, sausages, bacon, plates of fried potatoes. They ate ravenously; no food had ever tasted so good.

And there was plenty of drink. Some of the men uncapped bottles of stout and drank deeply in long swallows. Seamus Finn drained one bottle without taking it from his lips, then set it down empty with one hand and snatched up a full bottle with another. "Sure," he said, "and I'm going to hell in me Guinness." And he uncapped the second bottle and poured it down his throat.

Little Mick O'Sullivan, looking more like a leprechaun than ever, came over to them with a jug of colorless liquid. "Poteen," he announced. "Made not three miles from this very house, and none the worse for not having the tax paid on it."

David took a long drink, coughed, shivered, and passed her the jug. She tried a sip. It was very smooth but extremely strong, and it burned its way down her throat and into her stomach. She shook her head when O'Sullivan offered her another drink.

"It puts color in your cheeks, lass."

"Maybe later."

David took another drink, a longer one this time, and returned the jug to O'Sullivan without coughing. The little man beamed appreciatively. "It's a good lad you are," he said. "Ye'll have to teach the lass to drink. Though it can be bad if a woman develops too much of a taste for the jar. She'll turn her back on your housework and not be paying enough mind to the children."

She looked at David. His eyes met hers and she felt herself blushing. There were no more tears now, she thought: Only the elation of having survived and the joy of good fellowship. Warmth permeated the cottage, and only a portion of it emanated from the turf fire on the hearth. The greater part came from the men themselves.

"Oh, I feel like singing," she cried.

O'Sullivan had already told the others that Ellen was a singer. Now one of them came to her, a banjo in hand. She was not very good with the banjo, had only experimented with that instrument from time to time, but she sensed that the professionalism of her performance would not matter. She took the banjo, and they gathered around, jugs of poteen and bottles of stout in hand.

"What shall I sing?"

Suggestions came from every quarter, but Fergal O'Hara's voice overrode the others. "Give us a song for today," he said. "A song to commemorate the fighting by the caves."

"You mean make one up?"

"I do."

"I don't know if I can . . ."

"Then can ye play for me? And do you know the tune to 'The Men of the West'?"

She did; it was the same tune that was also used for "Acres of Clams" and "The Eighteenth Day of November" and several other ballads. She plucked tentatively at the banjo, letting her fingers accustom themselves to the unfamiliar tuning, then began to play the chords and, bit by bit, pick out the melody.

He let her go through two choruses to get used to the banjo. Then, in a sweet tenor voice as clear as a church-bell, he began to sing.

> *In the county of old Tipperary*
> *One night in the fall of the year*
> *The spawn of the devil came riding*
> *To gun down a lad and his dear*
>
> *But they never took into accounting*
> *The boys of the West Tip Brigade*
> *Who shot them with rifles and pistols*
> *And blew them to hell with grenades*

"Didn't use a solitary grenade," someone said. "Canister bombs and bottles of petrol, but not a grenade did we have." Someone else told him to hold his hour and have another, and passed him a jar of poteen.

> *Oh, they lay in the darkness in waiting*
> *Outside of the Mitchelstown Cave*

To fight for their master, bold Satan
And murder our Ellen and Dave

But Jamie was there with his pistol
And Fergal, and Mick, and both Seans
And Seamus and Peader and Tommy
To shoot 'em all dead before dawn

"Shoot 'em all dead in ten minutes," someone said.

So here's to the West Tipperary boys
So valiant and bold and serene
And here's to the Irish Republic—
Now pass me that jar of poteen!

They applauded wildly and made him sing it four more times, and each time he added another verse. And then they called for some of the other Republican songs—"Take It Down from the Mast" and "The Patriot Game" and "Barry's Column" and more, and she played them all and they sang them all, and the room rocked with their singing.

Hardly anyone noticed when the friar came in. There was knocking at the door, and Mrs. O'Hara scurried off to answer it. A robed form passed through from the doorway to the kitchen, and moments later Mrs. O'Hara returned to the room.

But Fergal said, "Who was it, Mother?"

"Oh, and only a friar, a poor Dominican, and him so chilled and wet and saying he hadn't eaten since yesterday morning. I've got him in the kitchen with a plate of food before him."

"And him wandering the countryside at this hour?"

"He was lost, he'd lost his way and saw our light on. The poor man, how cold and wet he was."

"Then he'll need more than food in him, Mother. Bring him in and pass him a jar."

"And if he doesn't drink?"

"And Mother, when did you know a Dominican who didn't?"

Mrs. O'Hara returned to the kitchen. She reappeared moments later with the friar at her side. He wore a great brown cloak with a hood covering his head, and he moved into the room smiling shyly, and Ellen glanced at him and looked at the banjo and then looked at him again, and her eyes rolled and she shrieked.

It was Farrell.

No one moved. Everyone stared at her, puzzled. She was the only one who recognized him, the only one who had ever seen him. And now, as her cry hung in the air, she watched as he reached into a fold in his cloak and drew out a small black automatic pistol—

Someone shouldered her aside, pushing through the crowd. David. The gun drew up and pointed at her, and David threw himself on Farrell. The gun went off. A bullet streaked upward and buried itself in the thatched roof. The two men thrashed on the floor, locked in furious combat. The gun discharged a second time, and a bullet flew across the crowded room, and a man cried out in sudden pain.

She watched, wide-eyed, breathless, her heart pounding furiously. Watched as David wrested the gun free and tossed it aside. Watched as his hands—his gentle hands, but gentle no longer—flailed at the false friar, beating him to the ground.

Watched as David got up, slowly, blood trickling from his nose, a bruise on one cheek. And watched as Farrell lay motionless upon the cottage floor.

There was a furious debate over what to do with Farrell. Peader Killeen suggested that they put a pistol bullet in his head and be done with it. Seamus Finn, who had taken one of Farrell's bullets in his right thigh, argued persuasively for beating his brains out with a pike. Jimmy Davis thought they ought to hang him.

"He's more use alive," David insisted.

"He's no use, alive or dead."

"Some people will have a lot of questions to ask him," David explained. "Questions he'll have to answer. And when they're done with him, he'll get what's coming to him. He killed a woman in Dingle and probably murdered a motorist on the road. And may have killed many more. What happens to murderers in Ireland?"

"They're sentenced to life in prison. It used to be the gallows for them, but now it's only prison."

"Then that's where he's going."

They felt cheated out of the chance for an execution but went along with it. They tied up the unconscious Farrell, lashed his wrists and ankles together, and locked him in a closet. Then they brought out more jars of poteen and more bottles of Guinness and another tray of food, and went on with the party.

Ellen picked her banjo and everyone sang. Twice more Fergal O'Hara had to go through "The Boys of the West Tip

Brigade," and on the second run-through he added a verse to include the night's latest development.

> *But the worst of the villains deceived us*
> *And lived to escape from the fray*
> *And garbed in the robes of a friar*
> *He came to O'Hara's that day*
>
> *But our own darling Ellen she spied him*
> *And David he wrestled him clean*
> *And the government's going to jail him—*
> *Now where in the hell's the poteen?*

Chapter 21

Farrell cracked wide-open the moment the police began their interrogation. Defeat, his first defeat, had been too much for him. Mentally unstable from the beginning, he was completely unhinged by defeat; he raved like a lunatic. Along with the raving he came out with the facts.

One fact, at least, fit with what he had originally told Ellen. He had spent several years in Africa, but not as a missionary. He was a free-lance spy and *agent provocateur* working to undermine various governments in independent Africa. In the course of his espionage he had come up with something big—a master list of all U.S. and British agents and sympathizers in one of the new African republics.

This information had been recorded upon the scrap of microfilm that he concealed in Ellen's passport. He planned to offer it for sale in Berlin and would have solicited bids from four governments—those of the United States, Britain, the Soviet Union, and Mainland China. Anyone attempting to overthrow the pro-Western government would have found the list invaluable; anyone wanting to maintain the government would pay well to keep it out of enemy hands.

A member of the U.S. Central Intelligence Agency received the microfilm from an agent of the Irish Government and took it back to Washington. Farrell—his real name, it turned out, was Henri Curtin, and he was a Belgian—was locked in a cell to await a trial that would send him to prison for life. The loose ends were tied up. The innocent victims— Sara Trevelyan, the man who had given Farrell a ride toward Dingle, another man shot by Koenig for an indeterminable reason—went to their separate graves. A garda named Patrick Daly had his motorcycle returned to him in acceptable condition. A man named Denis Mahoney received a C.I.A. check for one hundred pounds as compensation for seven full-grown sheep at seven pounds, ten shillings apiece, plus the balance for inconvenience and indignities suffered in the interest of the United States Government.

And Ellen Cameron missed the Berlin Folk Music Festival.

And now they were in Dublin again, where they had met and where the final stages of the interrogation had taken place. They had gone to O'Donohue's for the singing, but left before closing and found another quieter pub several blocks away. They sat alone in the small snug and sipped pints of stout.

He said, "Well, they'll clear up the problem of your passport in a day or two, I suppose. Issue you a new one. It would be nice if they let you keep the other for a souvenir, but I don't suppose they will."

"I guess not."

"You'll be glad to get the new passport, won't you?"

"I suppose I will."

"And I'm sure you'll be anxious to get back to New York.

You must have had enough of Ireland to last you for the rest of your life."

"Why do you say that?"

"Everything you went through . . ."

"How can you say that?" She was actually angry. "I met the nicest people in the world. The most wonderful people on earth. I had a grand trip. Dublin, and then the small towns on the way to Dingle, and Dingle itself. And the men in Tipperary, God, what wonderful men they were! And the singing, and the food and drink, and the warmth of everyone, and the scenery, and the air, so fresh and clean . . ."

"Don't forget the rain."

"I didn't mind the rain. I didn't melt, did I?"

"Not noticeably."

"And how could you think I could help being utterly in love with this country? Why? Because of a couple of horrible days? Because there are evil men in the world? Because I came a little close to getting killed? It wasn't Ireland's fault."

"You sound as though you like it here."

"I love it here!"

"And your eyes are funny. You're not going to cry, are you?"

"No, I'm not. I am not. Damn you, don't look at me, I can't help it, dammit. Oh, David . . ."

A little later she said, "I'm going to be forward, I can't help it. You know what brash things American girls are. And the first night in Dublin the cab driver said that all Americans are a little bit daft, so I'm sure you'll pardon my brashness—"

"Sure, and it's the way of you American colleens."

"—because I want to go to Connemara with you."

"Do you mean that?"

She nodded. "If you'll take me. If I wouldn't be in the way."

"You could never be in the way, Ellen." He took a deep swallow of the black stout. "Ellen? You must be a little homesick for New York. Anxious to see your friends and your agent and everyone. After all, it's your home, isn't it?"

"My home was a town called Belvedere, New Hampshire. The last time I went back was for my mother's funeral. I never went back again. I never will." She hesitated. "New York isn't home," she said. She thought of the crowds, the polluted air, the endless rushing around, the slums, the violence, the summer heat, the winter cold. The subways at rush hour, the harsh rudeness of strangers to strangers, the endless sensation of being trapped in a world of steel and glass and cement.

"New York was never home," she said, "and never could be home."

"Could Ireland?"

Her voice wouldn't work; something seemed to be stuck in her throat. She swallowed but it wouldn't go away.

"I was thinking," he said. "About Farrell—I mean Curtin, I keep calling him Farrell. His disguises. First a priest and then a friar."

She nodded.

"I hope it didn't leave you with a permanent fear of clergymen. Because I think the two of us ought to see one together one of these days. On the way to Connemara. Ellen . . ."

And then, with a little sob, she was in his arms. She tasted his mouth on hers, felt his strong arms around her, holding her tight.

I never shall marry
I'll be no man's wife

I'm bound to stay single
All the days of my life

Ah, but the song was a lie, a lie!

After a few moments she eased herself out of his arms. He reached for her again and she drew away.

"Someone will see us," she said.

"Not a chance."

"But we're in a pub, a public house . . ."

"Silly girl," he said. "Why do you think they call it a snug?"

She smiled a lazy smile. "How very clever of them," she said dreamily, "to call it a snug. For snuggling. How sweet!"

And then she went to him, and neither of them said anything for a long time.

My Newsletter: I get out an email newsletter at unpredictable intervals, but rarely more often than every other week. I'll be happy to add you to the distribution list. A blank email to lawbloc@gmail.com with "newsletter" in the subject line will get you on the list, and a click of the "Unsubscribe" link will get you off it, should you ultimately decide you're happier without it.

About the Author

Lawrence Block has been writing award-winning mystery and sus-
pense fiction for half a century. His newest book, a sequel to his
greatly successful Hopper anthology *In Sunlight or in Shadow*, is
Alive in Shape and Color, a 17-story anthology with each story il-
lustrated by a great painting; authors include Lee Child, Joyce Car-
ol Oates, Michael Connelly, Joe Lansdale, Jeffery Deaver and David
Morrell. His most recent novel, pitched by his Hollywood agent
as "James M. Cain on Viagra," is *The Girl with the Deep Blue Eyes*.
Other recent works of fiction include *The Burglar Who Counted
The Spoons*, featuring Bernie Rhodenbarr; *Keller's Fedora*, featuring
philatelist and assassin Keller; and *A Drop Of The Hard Stuff*, featuring Matthew Scudder, brilliantly embodied by Liam Neeson in
the 2014 film, *A Walk Among The Tombstones*. Several of his other
books have also been filmed, although not terribly well. He's well
known for his books for writers, including the classic *Telling Lies
For Fun & Profit* and *Write For Your Life*, and has recently published
a collection of his writings about the mystery genre and its practi-
tioners, *The Crime Of Our Lives*. In addition to prose works, he has
written episodic television (*Tilt!*) and the Wong Kar-wai film, *My
Blueberry Nights*. He is a modest and humble fellow, although you
would never guess as much from this biographical note.

Email: lawbloc@gmail.com
Twitter:@LawrenceBlock
Facebook: lawrence.block
Website: lawrenceblock.com